TALES FROM MANILA AVE.

Sundress Publications • Knoxville, TN

Copyright © 2025 by Patrick Joseph Caoile
ISBN: 978-1-951979-84-3
LCCN: 2025942841
Published by Sundress Publications
www.sundresspublications.com

Editor: Samantha Edmonds
Managing Editor: Krista Cox
Editorial Assistants: Sarah Harshbarger
Editorial Interns: Aylli Cortez, Kanika Lawton,
    Catie Macauley, Tassneem Abdulwahab

Colophon: This book is set in Cardo and Marion.
Cover Art: "Taking Flight" by Amyel Oliveros
Cover Design: Kristen Camille Ton
Book Design: Sarah Harshbarger and Krista Cox

TALES FROM MANILA AVE.

Patrick Joseph Caoile

ACKNOWLEDGMENTS

The following stories first appeared in these publications:

Bright Flash Literary Review, "Kapé"
Chestnut Review, "Tong, Tong, Tong"
Growing Up Filipino 3: New Stories for Young Adults, ed. Cecilia Manguerra Brainard (PALH, 2023 / UST Publishing House, 2022), "Dress Down Day"
Solstice Literary Magazine, "Tales from Manila Ave."
storySouth, "A State of Grace" as "A State Of."

A version of this manuscript was recognized as a semifinalist in the 2023 Autumn House Prize in Fiction.

TABLE OF CONTENTS

To the Caoiles and Cayabyabs in the Philippines, United States, and elsewhere, in this world and the next.

TALES FROM MANILA AVE.

People often disappeared from our apartment building on Manila Ave. At least that's what Kuya Jem used to tell us. He wasn't really our brother. That's just what everyone in our building called him—Kuya. He did a lot of things for us and the other tenants. In the morning, he tended to the halaman planted in pots along the front of our building. We woke up to his singing, his karaoke rendition of Elvis Presley's "Can't Help Falling in Love," while the early birds chirped along. While we waited for the school bus to arrive, we watched him talk to the plants. "You just need a little more sun," Kuya Jem said to a budding bunch of tulips. He gradually moved the pot farther out, towards the sidewalk, where the perfect amount of light hit it, abiding by the sun's hourly procession. When we boarded the bus, he waved after us, saying, "Study hard, hah! Make your parents proud!" That was a nice way to start the day. We did our best.

During the day, Kuya Jem went from gardener to handyman. The landlord was almost never around, so Kuya Jem took maintenance requests straight from the residents. He didn't mind. He was friendly that way, and everyone in the building knew he could be trusted. He had one of those faces, almost forever young. He had plump cheeks and a wide smile that brought out his dimples. He couldn't have been older than thirty, but he carried himself like an elder, a veteran resident of Manila Ave. There was something of the countryman in him, as if his love for plants and gardening grew out of a childhood on a farm. Whenever he knocked on a tenant's door, he was received warmly. He took up their hand and raised it to his forehead and said, "Mano po." We usually only received blessings from people older than us—aunts, uncles, friends of our parents. But Kuya Jem was well-blessed by everyone, even by some of the younger residents, newer ones who moved in for the easy commute into the city. The Filipino residents took it as a custom, and those who weren't Filipino were endeared. In those days, everyone knew Kuya Jem, and he knew just about everyone.

We always looked forward to Friday nights, when our little neighborhood on Manila Ave. gathered in the backyard of our building and Kuya Jem would tell us his stories. Many of the tenants would plan an end-of-the-week potluck. Most were Filipino dishes, which meant many of our fried favorites: lumpia, lechon kawali, turon. We delighted in anything golden brown that crunched in our mouths. That also applied to the other tenants' dishes. One family brought empanadas of many kinds—beef, pulled pork, guava and cheese—all their greasy fillings dripping down our chins. Another family brought fried chicken wings, which we were warned were spicy and not made for our delicate taste buds. But we were stubborn little kids with no inhibitions. Afterward, we doused our tongues in buko juice.

After each family had their fill, our parents sat around in lawn chairs. Our fathers with beer bottles in hand, our mothers with indignant stares. They discussed the neighborhood tsismis—the new young couple who moved into the first floor whom they suspected were runaway high school sweethearts; the rumors of Hank's Deli on the corner closing down due to a rat infestation; and, of course, the latest disappearance on Manila Ave. And while their stories could have been more accurate, we had no care for nor sense of the absolute truth. Back then, all that mattered to us was Kuya Jem's version of the truth, the way he bent it towards magic.

He'd sit on a tree stump and beckon us all to some small patch of grass. We followed, asking for his blessing—"mano po"—and sat cross-legged knee-to-knee, more well-behaved than we were in school.

It would still be light out, the sunset some minutes away. But already the fireflies were flickering. It was the perfect setting for the storyteller. Maybe it was the evening light, the way the strong shadows struck his plump, round face revealing new angles, but Kuya Jem no longer resembled the morning gardener who wished us well before we got on the bus. To us, on those Friday evenings huddled in the grass, Kuya Jem was a preacher reading gospel. He would always begin with a question.

★

"Has anyone seen Manong Manuel lately?" Kuya Jem asked.

Whispers spread among us, heads shaking, *Have you? No, have you?*

We all knew who he was. Manong Manuel lived on the fourth floor, but he was also a math teacher at the high school, so we didn't look forward to high school. We were scared of him. He was balding beyond repair, a few combed-over strands feathering his scalp. Whenever he blinked, his right eye lagged behind his left, so we never looked at him up close, careful not to be struck by his odd, asymmetrical stare. He also walked with a cane that helped him with his limp. Some of us who were older had heard from the high school students that Manong Manuel—Mr. Burgos, as he was known at the school—was one of the strictest teachers they had. He would fail any student who tried to look him straight in the eyes. He was a boogeyman living in our apartment building. We would have never thought that Manong Manuel was anything otherwise.

I heard he ate squirrels for breakfast! one of us said.

He gave my brother detention in a dungeon one time, another one said.

"No, no, no," Kuya Jem said with authority, dispelling our own little tales about Manong Manuel. "Manong Manuel didn't do any of those things."

He read the confusion on our faces.

"Hm, puwes," he continued. "Does anyone know what an OFW is?"

Those younger tried to sound it out as if the acronym were a full word, while the rest of us waited for the answer.

"OFW stands for Ogre-Fighting-Warrior. Now I'm sure you all know what an ogre is."

A monster! That one we knew. *A monster from the swamp!*

"Yes!" He began to change his face, forcing his eyes open like bullseyes, mangling his mouth, inhaling one cheek so half his face looked lifeless. He stood up, brought his back forward into a hunch, and curled his fingers into claws. He let out a gurgling sound under his breath, then pretended to lunge at one of us in the front row. We screamed with genuine fear, then—as Kuya Jem returned to his tree stump, the storyteller once again—we began to laugh at one another's squeamishness.

"Ogres are monsters that live in swamps. They're some of the most terrifying aswangs around. But sometimes...they leave the swamp. Sometimes... they find you.

"I met Manong Manuel before any of you were born," he continued. "I knew him when he was a young man in the Philippines. I was one of his first math students, and I also called him 'Mr. Burgos.' Back then, he walked perfectly fine, and his eyesight was as sharp as a shooter. Like you, we were scared to have him as a teacher. He was strict and wanted us to behave. Really, none of us liked math very much. But we did our best. Mr. Burgos made sure of it. A lot of us stayed after school for his tutoring, especially after a test we all failed. Of course, our parents made us go, too. But we didn't mind staying after school. We wanted to know what happened at school when classes ended. And one day, we got what we asked for.

"It was a stormy afternoon. The sky rumbled, the thunder roared. 'Stay away from the windows,' Mr. Burgos warned. The rainwater was spilling over the roof and over the glass. We thought it was a typhoon. What we didn't know was that it was during storms like this when ogres left their swamps and found their way into our neighbor-hoods."

BOOM, BOOM, BOOM. Kuya Jem stomped his foot against the dry dirt. We felt the ground tremble against his work boot, each step landing with the strength of an ogre, flecks of soil flying through the air.

"The ogre's footsteps echoed through the hallways. They were louder than the thunder. But Mr. Burgos told us not to worry. 'Ogres are my specialty,' he told us. Hah! He was so cool back then—astig na astig. He told us to crouch under our desks and stay put until he got back. He opened the door and peered into the hallway. We shook as we heard the loud moaning of the ogre. Mr. Burgos addressed us one more time—'I'll be right back'—then walked out into the hallway and shut the door.

BOOM, BOOM, BOOM. "We heard the ogre walk towards Mr. Burgos. Its footsteps grew faster and louder." *BOOMBOOMBOOMBOOM.* "Like a stampede of carabao. But just before we thought it would get to Mr. Burgos, the ogre's steps went silent. We heard Mr. Burgos shout, 'Ya!' followed by a whimpering. Then, a loud thud. We were still curled up beneath our desks, still so afraid, when Mr. Burgos came back for us. 'Come,' he said, 'come and see.' So we followed him out to the hallway.

"The ogre was ten feet in height," Kuya Jem said, standing on top of the tree stump for scale. "Its skin was green as the grass, its teeth sharp as a dog's. But it was dead. Mr. Burgos—Manong Manuel—had killed it with merely his fists. On the ogre's forehead was a giant, swollen lump."

Still standing tall, Kuya Jem mimicked a boxer's pose, then jabbed the air in front of him in a swift motion. "In one punch, Mr. Burgos defeated the ogre. He was the Manny Pacquiao of Ogre-Fighting-Warriors!"

Kuya Jem concluded the story with how Mr. Burgos became Manong Manuel. After years and years of fighting ogres in the Philippines, Mr. Burgos came to fight American ogres. He was still the best OFW around, but his fights began taking their toll on his body. After so many brawls, his eyesight waned. He suffered a number of injuries, which led to his use of a cane. But when Kuya Jem eventually moved to America and found out that Mr. Burgos was still fighting ogres, he convinced the old man to stop. "He was a great teacher after all," Kuya Jem explained, "and there were still many students who needed him. I called him Manong because he was like an older brother to me and others. He was our hero. But now he's also getting very old to teach, and he misses home. When he arrives back in the Philippines, he'll have a hero's welcome!"

All this time we thought Manong Manuel was the monster, hunched over on a cane with disgruntled eyes. We had no idea we were in the presence of a hero.

After Kuya Jem finished his tale, we joined the adults for a toast. They held up their beers while we held up our cans of buko juice. "To Manong Manuel," our parents shouted.

To Manong Manuel, we echoed.

Later, we asked our parents whether he was really an OFW. "Yes, he is," they assured us. "But he's retired back in the Philippines."

So we believed Kuya Jem's story. We regretted not having known before, but then we began to celebrate the acclaimed OFW in our own way. Some of us pretended to be ogres, running around the backyard. One of us would play the role of Manong Manuel, chasing ogres until not one of us was left untagged. That's how it was for all of Kuya Jem's stories. They became a part of our lives as the children of Manila Ave. We let our imaginations run wild on our little block. It was like that until the Percivals arrived and moved into our building.

★

Martin Percival appeared one morning as we waited for the school bus. It was Kuya Jem who introduced us to Manila Ave.'s newest resident. He was Filipino, like many of us, but different. Just by the way he dressed, we knew. While we wore simple jeans and T-shirts, Martin had on a white polo tucked into khaki pants. He had on a uniform because, unlike us, he went to St. Anthony's, the Catholic private school where the better-off kids went. That explained why he was waiting by himself some distance away from us. But Kuya Jem took a break from his morning gardening routine to call him over to us. "Martin," he said. "Come meet some friends." Martin hesitated, but after Kuya Jem's insistence—and our awkward, prying stares—he joined us.

"Mga kaibigan," Kuya Jem called us. "This is Martin Percival. He and his father just moved into the top floor. Everyone say hi to Martin."

Hi, Martin, we said.

"He goes to school at St. Anthony's, isn't that right, Martin?"

"Opo," Martin said.

"But that doesn't make him any different from me or you guys. So make sure to treat him like one of us."

Yes, Kuya Jem. We looked at one another and nodded. One of us took Martin by his hand. *You can wait here with us, too!*

"Good, good," Kuya Jem said.

Martin looked uncomfortable. We had only just met him, yet we were already eager to have him join us. We all knew what it was like being the new kid at school, so we made sure that the new kids like Martin weren't so new for too long. It was easier for the Filipino boys and girls—their parents practically forced us to become friends. We ended up calling each other's parents titos and titas, not bonded by blood but by home country instead. For those of us who weren't Filipino, it was a little harder. But they eventually warmed up to us—their parents, though not Filipino, also came from countries elsewhere. We all had that in common, immigrant families looking for a sense of community in an American city. We made Manila Ave. that community, our own little world. And at its center was Kuya Jem.

"And Martin," he added, "make sure to tell your tatay that we'll be having a party in the backyard this Friday. It's a big party with lots of food and games."

And stories! we exclaimed. *Kuya Jem tells the best stories!*

"Stories?" Martin asked. "What kind of stories?"

"You'll just have to come to the party to find out," Kuya Jem said with a warm smile. Then, he returned to his singing—ABBA's "Chiquitita"—and his tulips.

Martin's ride came first. To our surprise, it wasn't a school bus that picked him up and brought him to school. It was a sleek, black luxury car with a driver. Some of us gasped as we watched Martin walk to the car. But Kuya Jem was unphased. He gave Martin the same instructions as he always gave us. "Study hard, Martin! And make your father proud!" We watched the car speed off Manila Ave. and we waited for our own school bus to arrive.

★

That Friday, everyone gathered in the backyard for the potluck party. It was still too early for the festivities to begin. The adults were setting up the picnic tables and chairs, carrying around their steaming trays of pancit and rice, pernil and maduros, and even lasagna—though it had a layer of tuna in it. To keep us away from the food, our parents encouraged us to go play in the grass. We were in the middle of playing Manong versus Ogres when Martin sauntered over.

Come play with us, we called. *Do you want to be Manong Manuel?*

"Manong Manuel?"

Kuya Jem told us about him. He's an Ogre-Fighting-Warrior!

"My dad says not to listen to Kuya Jem," Martin said. "My dad says to stay away from him." This confused us. We stopped chasing each other and gathered around Martin.

What do you mean?

"My dad says Kuya Jem is an alien. He says he doesn't belong here. That he got here the wrong way and he didn't do it the right way like we did."

Kuya Jem isn't an alien! We looked at each other and found the same puzzled expressions. We didn't know what Martin was talking about, but we did know Kuya Jem. *Kuya Jem is cool! Kuya Jem is the best! He's our friend!*

We had started yelling at Martin, whose eyes began to water.

"Hoy!" Kuya Jem said as he ran towards us. "What's going on here?" Kuya Jem approached him, but the boy backed away from him and the rest of us. We kept silent.

"Itigil nyo na, okay? That's enough." He looked at us. We nodded. He looked at Martin, who also nodded. "The food is ready anyway. Kain na!"

We followed Kuya Jem to the food tables, but he gestured for us to wait. He called Martin over to the front of the line.

"Where's your father?" he whispered.

"Still at work," Martin said.

"Hm…well, because you're our newest resident, you can have the first plate."

We watched as Martin piled each dish onto his plate, as if he had never eaten before. From the lumpia to the empanadas, lasagna to pancit, his plate was stacked with all things crispy, juicy, and saucy. "Alright, now everybody can eat!" Kuya Jem announced. We cheered and followed Martin's example—each plate a culinary Tower of Babel. We took our plates to Kuya Jem's stage, the patches of grass around his storytelling tree stump. Martin sat all the way behind us, content with his plate yet still wary of the so-called alien seated in front of us. After a few more bites, our stomachs almost at capacity, Kuya Jem began his new tale.

★

"Has anyone seen Miss Guadalupe lately?"

No, we said, not one of us recalling the last time we saw her. Miss Guadalupe was a beautiful woman who lived on the first floor. She had been one of the newer residents, though she made herself comfortable in the building and among the others. It was her pancit that everyone craved; no one dared rival hers with their own recipe. But she remained humble. She was still young, addressing the rest of the tenants as "sir," "mam," and "po." She worked as a day nanny in the city, taking care of rich people's children while they made rich people money. But she enjoyed her job. Her bright, rosy cheeks greeted us every time she passed by. "Are you listening to your parents?" she'd ask. *Yes, po.* "Are you listening to Kuya Jem?" she followed up. *Yes, po.* We loved her, everyone did. She woke up earlier than the other residents, only second to Kuya Jem who began his maintenance duties just before dawn. There were rumors that the two of them were lovers. We had rooted for the couple. But if they were together, neither made it obvious. Only in their occasional glances passing through the halls of our apartment building on Manila Ave.

Is she gone? We started to panic. *Why did she leave? She was so nice to us!*

"She isn't gone," Kuya Jem said. "But she has left," he admitted, a frown flashed on his face.

"Miss Guadalupe has fallen in love!" he explained. "Miss Guadalupe has fallen in love with a Canadian prince."

Canadian? We were enthralled by this prince. To our naive ears, Canadian sounded fancy. We had never heard of Canada at that age, or at the very least, confused Canada for some faraway fairytale land rather than our northern neighbor. *Does that make her a Canadian princess?* we asked.

"Yes," Kuya Jem said. "Princesa Guadalupe Barbeau, beautiful wife to Prince Bob Barbeau, and heiress to the Canadian throne. But she almost didn't become a princess. Prince Barbeau had a rival to Miss Guadalupe's hand in marriage. Prince Jerome of Pampanga!" He stood up on his tree stump, one hand on his hip and the other gripping an imaginary sword, ready to duel. We clapped and cheered for Prince Jerome. "Hear, hear! Give it up for the Prinsipe of Pampanga!"

Hear, hear! Hear, hear! we shouted. Kuya Jem clutched his hands on top of another, conjuring a trumpet out of thin air, *DAH DATATAH!*

"It is I who will win Miss Guadalupe's heart," Kuya Jem, as Jerome, said. "Siya ang aking pagibig!"

He turned his body the other way, reversing his knightly stance.

"No, no," Kuya Jem said, this time with an attempt at a Canadian accent, which was more like French. "I am Prince Bob Barbeau, heir to

23

the kingdom of Canada, and the true heir to Lady Guadalupe's heart!"

He flipped his body again, returning to his part as Prince Jerome.

"Then let us fight!" And the duel commenced. Kuya Jem took turns being Jerome and Bob Barbeau, shifting his body in odd angles for our entertainment. He swung high, then ducked low. He jabbed forward, then jumped backwards. We continued to cheer and even gasped at the drama, the tragic tale of romance and jealousy. "YAH!" the Pampangan prince shouted. "Take that!" the Canadian prince rebutted. Kuya Jem did all this on his single tree stump, and while he had done well to keep his balance during the performance, he finally lost his footing and fell to the ground. *Oh no!* we exclaimed. "If this is over," he continued, "then at least I would have died for love." Though we knew who was the victor, we held onto our breaths, guessing at which part he was playing, which prince had fallen. Still on the ground, Kuya Jem shouted to the heavens, "Miss Guadalupe! You will always be my...mahal." With his last word of love, Prince Jerome of Pampanga laid still in the dirt, his eyes closed, and his heart broken.

★

"Get away from my son!" a stranger shouted behind us.

Kuya Jem ended his performance and was starting to get back up.

"I said get away from my son," the stranger said. "Martin, come here now! I told you to keep away from him."

We knew then that the man was Martin's father, Mr. Percival. He wore a navy-blue suit, shirt and tie and all. His hair was slicked back with a greasy gel, and a moustache grazed his upper lip. His thick eyebrows pointed in diagonals, the wrinkles on his forehead squished together. This was the same man who had told Martin that Kuya Jem was an alien.

"Mr. Percival, sir." Kuya Jem put his hand out to greet him. It was still covered in dirt from the fall he took as Prince Jerome.

Mr. Percival refused the greeting by slapping Kuya Jem's hand away.

"Stay away from me and my son," he shouted. "Stay away or I'll make you disappear! You and the rest of them!" He took Martin by the hand and led him back into the apartment building. We heard Mr. Percival's footsteps through the hallway and up the stairs, even as we were still outside, shaken by the scene. Our parents put down their drinks and ceased gossiping. Their eyes darted between each other until they finally looked towards Kuya Jem. He kept a still, stoic countenance, unmoved by Mr. Percival's harsh words. We could hear Martin crying: "I'm sorry, Dad. I'm sorry."

After a few minutes, the Percivals reached their apartment, and we couldn't hear them anymore—only the clicking of the nighttime bugs signaling the day's end.

"It's getting late," Kuya Jem said, breaking the silence. After Mr. Percival's tirade, the party was clearly over. Our parents wrapped up the party trays of food, others took whatever leftovers they could fit onto paper plates. "Magandang gabi, everyone," Kuya Jem said, then began to help the other adults fold up the picnic chairs and tables. It was an abrupt, somber end to our Friday night.

That night, before we had fallen asleep, the thought of Mr. Percival's threat kept our minds running. What did it mean that he'd send Kuya Jem away? How could he do such a thing? We knew how people from Manila Ave. often disappeared. But we never thought Kuya Jem could be one of them. It was his duty to tell us about the disappearances, not to disappear himself, not to become one of his own stories and leave no one else to tell it.

★

The morning Kuya Jem disappeared began like any other day, though young Martin Percival was nowhere to be seen. None of us had seen him since his father's outburst the Friday before. It was the start of a new week, and since Kuya Jem was whistling and singing to the tulips as usual, it seemed like nothing had changed. This time he sang Frank Sinatra's "New York, New York." The birds chirped along as always—even they didn't know it would be his last song sung on Manila Ave.

When we waited outside for the school bus to arrive, Kuya Jem held up a hand for some high-fives. "Apir!" he said. He held up his hand slightly higher than our reach, but we all jumped for it and made it. "Yes! Yes! And yes! The higher you jump, the taller you'll grow. Just like these flowers, you should all reach for the sun." We believed him. We continued to take turns jumping for his hand, one apir after the other, thinking we'd grow to great heights, tall enough to face any ogre, monster, or alien. The school bus eventually arrived, and we had to leave Kuya Jem to tend to the rest of his plants. He waved goodbye, his palm now red from our high-fives. Still, he smiled, dimple to dimple. Still, he told us, "Study hard, hah! Make your parents proud!"

When we came back at the end of our school day, Kuya Jem was nowhere to be found. The residents were in a panic. Surely they knew more about his disappearance than we did. Though it wasn't a Friday, no potluck to plan and set up, the adults gathered out back and let us play around that evening. But we were in no mood to play— we also wanted to know what had happened to

Kuya Jem. Even without his presence, we came together because of him.

"It was Mr. Percival," we overheard one of our parents say. "He put in the call, and they came after him during the day."

"Walang hiya siya," another parent said in frustration.

We were surprised to see that the landlord—his bald head dripping sweat, his eyes refusing to meet anyone else's—had joined them too, perhaps to give some sort of explanation. We heard Mr. Percival's name repeated, even Martin came up in their heated conversation. "I can't do anything about it," the landlord concluded. "And I've already sold the building to him. He'll be in charge in just a few weeks." He brushed his palms together as if to wash them clean, then threw them into the air. But our parents continued to berate him.

Meanwhile, we had our own debates. *Was Martin right? Is Kuya Jem an alien?* we asked one another. *Maybe he went back to the others like him.* We mulled over the theory but weren't satisfied. *He isn't an alien. He's just like us! What does Martin know about Kuya Jem anyway? We've known him longer.* There was no point in arguing. Kuya Jem had been family to us—the eccentric uncle with eccentric stories to tell. Nothing could have shaken our faith in him and our belief in his stories. We all agreed Kuya Jem had more in common with us than some green, googly-eyed extraterrestrial.

★

We didn't see Martin Percival much in the weeks after Kuya Jem left. His father must have kept him cooped up in their top floor apartment, away from the rest of us who helped shelter an apparent alien. We knew Martin was still around, that he still went to St. Anthony's Catholic school. From our apartment windows, we watched the same black luxury car and chauffeur pick him up in the morning. Martin came out in his white polo and khakis, alone. Because Kuya Jem was no longer there to wait with us, no longer there to sing to his halaman, we stayed in our apartments until we saw the school bus pull up outside. We still tried to study hard, just as Kuya Jem told us. We tried to make our parents proud. But it was harder without him.

Mr. Percival, who became the new property owner, began making some long overdue renovations. A new laundry room, a smoother elevator ride. Everyone knew the upgrades weren't necessarily for us but for the potential new residents that Mr. Percival wanted. We watched these strangers pass through the lobby, families with bright smiles and auras. *Are we getting new neighbors?* we asked our parents. But they merely groaned and rolled their eyes. Still, we looked forward to some new friends to join us, new players in our game of Manong Manuel versus Ogres. When some prospective families brought their children to an open house, we'd huddle behind the lobby desk and watch them eagerly. We waved to them, and once they noticed us, they often smiled back. But when Mr. Percival saw us, he'd rush over and tell us to go back to our apartments. "Or I'll make you disappear like Kuya Jem," he threatened. That scared us enough.

But we still had our Friday night gatherings. Not even Mr. Percival could stop us then. He would occasionally come out of his top floor apartment to reprimand the adults for having the music too loud. "Some neighbors have been complaining," he asserted, putting on some professional bravado in his navy-blue suit. No one believed him. Just about every resident of Manila Ave. had made their way to our potluck throughout the years, and they knew that the only resident complaining was Mr. Percival himself. They laughed behind his back as soon as he retreated into the building. Then the singing recommenced, the gossip spilled, the concert of our little barangay broadcast throughout the city. "Tagay!" they exclaimed, beer bottles in hand. *Tagay*, we echoed with our cans of buko juice.

During one of our gatherings, Martin came out of the building and surprised us outside. "I'm sorry about Kuya Jem," he said. *Do you know what happened to him?* we asked. "He went back to the Philippines where he belongs," he responded, though in our minds we knew those were Mr. Percival's words. We asked if he wanted to join us, to stay around for food and play our games. Though his eyes perked up at our offer, his frown displayed his restraint. "My Dad will be back soon," he explained. "I have to go." We watched him dart away with his head hung low. We wanted to chase after him, but feared his father as much as he did. Years later, when some of us would reminisce about our time on Manila Ave., we'd bring up Martin Percival and wonder what had happened to him, whether he eventually escaped his father and his ivory tower. We never did blame him for Kuya Jem's disappearance; admittedly, we felt bad for him.

Did Kuya Jem go back to the Philippines? we later asked our parents.

"Yes," they answered. "At least he's back home."

Knowing he was there comforted us. Maybe he was spending time with Manong Manuel, living out the heroic stories he used to tell us. Maybe he was just happy to be back home, where many of our own families were from.

Mr. Percival hired a new maintenance man for our building, but he had no care for singing, focused on his work rather than people, and showed no affinity for storytelling. He was merely Nick the maintenance man. If Kuya Jem were around, he would have conjured a story for him. We couldn't have lived up to his talents, so we didn't bother telling our own tales about him, or anyone for that matter. So Nick was merely Nick, and we were left to play and reenact the same stories, the ones Kuya Jem left us with. Though, as time went on, details changed. Instead of Manong Manuel fighting ogres, he fought vampires. Instead of Miss Guadalupe marrying a Canadian Prince, she was kidnapped by a Scandinavian pirate. We mixed and matched heroes and monsters, myths and legends. Kuya Jem gave us the tools, but we weren't master builders like him, capable of spontaneous creation. We did our best.

Eventually, when we got older and our imaginations were stifled by the facts of life and growing up, we left that apartment building on Manila Ave. One by one, we said our goodbyes. We became teenagers in high school, and the older ones left for college. Some of us moved out of state, others remained in various neighborhoods of the city. As our Friday potlucks got smaller, the tulips out front grew limp. Then the rent got too expensive, and more and more families like the Percivals moved in. The neighborhood was changing, and we couldn't keep up. It was as if, without Kuya Jem, Manila Ave. fell apart. Perhaps, when he had asked the residents "mano po," it was he who was blessing them, and us, and our community. He kept us together with his stories. Now there were no more stories to tell.

Except for the story of Kuya Jem. We told it no matter where we went. *Study hard. Reach for the sun. Pay attention to how someone acts, not how they look.* These were the lessons we strived to teach our own children. When our children reached the age we had been, all those years ago, we told them about Kuya Jem and his tales from Manila Ave.—how he inspired us to do our best, how he filled us with a sense of belonging where we might not have belonged, how he taught us what it meant to be good and kind. We told them the tale of Kuya Jem, the master storyteller who kept magic alive for the children of parents in search of a dream.

THE HOUSE AT THE END
OF MAPLEWOOOD DRIVE

While her mother reprimands her at the dinner table for showing *A Nightmare on Elm Street* to the two boys she babysits with her sister, Marie tries her best not to blame Anna. Though it was Anna's idea to bring along the film they had borrowed from the public library, Marie knows that her mother won't care, that she would merely let her know that, as the older sister, she should have known better than to show an R-rated 80s film to the newly immigrated boys who were about to experience their first American Halloween. "I had to hear it from their mother after church this morning," her mother says. "They couldn't sleep at all over the weekend." The Filipino mothers, lolas, and titas of Maplewood Drive and the surrounding neighborhood had formed a tight-knit community of Catholic women, those who not only moved to the States for better opportunities for their children but who would also do anything to guarantee their place alongside themselves in paradise when they passed into the next life. They wanted nothing to do with the wise-cracking child killer Freddy Krueger wreaking havoc in the dreams of teenagers in an idyllic American suburb. Maplewood Drive was no Elm Street. These women immigrated for dreams, not nightmares.

"Alright, I get it," says Marie. Though her words are meant for her mother, her stern stare is directed towards Anna. Anna rolls her eyes, not a word about the matter. "It won't happen again," Marie says.

"They look up to you, you know," her mother continues. "Those boys have come here younger than you." But her mother is wrong. Angelo and Daniel don't look up to *them*. The boys look up to Anna, the cool one, not her.

Marie was fourteen when they arrived from the Philippines. Anna was thirteen. Although they had been in the same grade together all their lives, Marie was placed in the tenth grade while Anna was placed in the ninth—something to do with the months their birthdays fell in, the school secretary explained. So, while Marie entered sophomore year as the new kid, Anna had a chance to start fresh entirely. It also didn't help that Marie was the "quiet one." As a young girl, she would sit in the shady corner of the yard while the other kids played tag. "Is your sister allergic to the sun?" Marie overheard another kid ask Anna, who had noticeably darker skin than Marie.

"No," Anna answered, "She's just that way." Marie buried herself in komiks instead. On the plane to the States, she carried her prized possessions: a collection of issues from her favorite superheroine Darna. On the other hand, Anna grew up with an affinity for performance. By the time she was eight, there wasn't a song she could not sing word for word from *Singin' in the Rain* or *The Sound of Music*. At the airport in Manila, Anna couldn't help but sing "So Long, Farewell" to their aunts and uncles before boarding the plane to America. She borrowed more from Julie Andrew's British accent when she spoke English, but then easily adapted to her classmates' American accents.

"Where are you going?" their mother says. Anna had finished her dinner in a rush.

"Sarah invited me over," Anna says, "to study." Marie knows that her sister has no intention of studying. Their mother doesn't know that Anna has been seeing Kevin, Sarah's older brother who is a senior at their high school. Whenever Anna went to Sarah's house to study, the only subjects she took seriously were Kevin's eyes and lips.

"Marie, go with your sister."

Their mother always turned Marie into her sister's personal chaperone. She would have much rather stayed home to study on her own—she truthfully had to study for a U.S. history test the next day. But Marie always complies with her mother's wishes. She is after all "Ate," and older sisters listen to their mothers and look after their siblings.

"I don't need a babysitter," Anna complains.

"Your Ate needs friends," their mother says. Marie glares at her mother, though she doesn't see.

"Sarah is *my* friend," Anna says.

"You can share."

Their mother gets the final word.

Marie hasn't even finished her dinner, a plate still half-full of rice and stewed mungo beans. But her sister already has her backpack over her shoulder and sneakers on her feet, halfway out the door, pouting through it all. *Such a drama queen,* Marie thinks. *Not everything revolves around you.* She quickly packs up her history textbook and joins her sister outside. On the walk to Sarah's, they remain silent. Marie wants to tell her sister to be grateful to her for taking all the blame about showing Angelo and Daniel *A Nightmare on Elm Street.* A block before Sarah's house, Anna stops her sister. "You really don't have to come with me. You'll just sit there watching us. Why don't you go somewhere else?"

"You think Mom will let it slide if she finds out I left you?"

"I won't tell. She won't even know," Anna says. "I know you don't want to be here."

Marie thinks it over. She doesn't want to be the third wheel to Anna and Kevin. She also isn't really friends with Sarah either. Whenever she's with Anna and her friends, Marie spends her time looking at her cell phone, searching for Darna fanart on online forums. She figures she can leave Anna just this one time. After all, it was Sarah's house and not the shopping mall. There would be no imminent danger—apart from Kevin. Marie knows that their mother's judgment hangs over both of them like the eyes of God. Anna wouldn't dare get into trouble with a boy, lest their mother conjure a flood to destroy the entire town as punishment.

"I'll be back at seven."

"Eight," Anna counters.

"Fine." It's five at the moment, and with three hours to spare, Marie thinks of walking to the public library where she can actually study for her test. Better to study there than at Sarah's where all she'd be focused on is not vomiting at the sight of her sister making out with her boyfriend.

*

Maplewood Drive is covered in Halloween. Inflatable jack-o-lanterns as big as refrigerators. Skeletons like those of giants stalked the sidewalks. Gnarly limbs protrude from the soil of front yards. When their family first moved into the neighborhood, both Marie and Anna were taken aback by how similar the ranch-style houses looked to each other. Brown roofs over off-white bases. The only differentiating detail seemed to be the numbers on the mailboxes. Not even the gated communities on the outer borders of Metro Manila quite looked like their new neighborhood. They had lived in one of those communities before immigrating. Each house there had been independently bought and constructed, unlike the uniform setting of their new American neighborhood. But this was where many of the Filipinos were moving. Marie's parents were among the new cohort of teachers recruited to fill the need of the local public schools, and there were other Filipinos who had come before. "It looks like a Hollywood set," Anna had said. *Cardboard houses* were what Marie had in mind. Now the street looks like it was plucked out from the Halloween episode of *The Brady Bunch*.

As realistic as the corpses, puppets, and other creatures look, Marie is not afraid. She grew up reading Darna komiks, stories about the Philippine superheroine with super strength, speed, and magical powers. One of Darna's nemeses was Valentina, a Medusa-like supervillain with snakes for her hair. Marie was well acquainted with stories of the gruesome, the grotesque, and the power of evil. Even when she watched *A Nightmare on Elm Street* with her sister and the boys, Marie never flinched. Not from Freddy Krueger's burnt and mangled face. Not from his sharp metallic claws. Not from his absurd shapeshifting abilities. If Freddy ever came across Darna, she would use her magical, extraterrestrial space stone to obliterate his crusty, snotty face. Her sister didn't pick up komiks the way she did. So, while they watched the horror movie, Anna was just as scared as the fifth-grade boys covering their faces underneath throw pillows on the couch. While Marie had been thinking of making her own Darna costume for Halloween, Anna had decided to dress like Heather Langenkamp's eighties final girl Nancy Thompson. She dragged Marie to the thrift store to look for pastel-colored tops and to the hair salon to style her hair into long, voluminous waves. Her boyfriend Kevin, of course, loved it. But maybe that's part of the reason her sister has had an easier time fitting in at school: Anna is willing to change.

The row of identical houses ends abruptly as Maplewood Drive gradually intersects with Main Street. Marie is about to make the turn when she hears a screeching sound, some animal's piercing outcry. The screeching comes from a wall of trees and shrubbery bordering the sidewalk, where a yard should have been. Marie, who wouldn't walk away from a helpless animal much like her komiks idol, crouches and peers through the bushes and branches for any sign of life. It doesn't take long for her eyes to locate the source of the sound. Inside is an animal that seems to glow in the dark. When her eyes adjust, Marie realizes that it isn't some radioactive rodent but a cat, so purely white it stands out from the shrubbery's shadow. Its eyes, too, pierce through the dark.

"Hey, kitty, kitty, kitty," Marie says. There were plenty of stray cats in the Philippines, though her parents always warned her and Anna to stay away, citing fleas and parasites. But this cat has a collar with a tag, which she can't make out in the dark just yet. She clicks her tongue against the roof of her mouth. "Come here," she says.

It doesn't budge but continues instead to meow in pain. Its eyes reflect whatever light reaches inside the bush, which isn't much. Yet the cat's glowing stare intensifies.

"Okay, okay." She bends lower to get under some branches, trying to break into the canopy. Urged on by the cat's incessant cries, Marie manages to make it into the opening. She squats closer to it, holding out her hand slowly. The cat welcomes the gesture and momentarily stops its screaming. With a much better look, Marie sees its paw stuck in a bundle of thorns. She takes the paw in one hand and uses the other to bend each thorn away. She feels each prick as she tries to free the cat, specks of blood appearing around her fingers. Marie, however, is unbothered. When the paw is completely free, she brushes her hands against her jeans. The cat comes out slowly, not afraid.

"You're welcome," Marie says. The cat brushes its face against Marie's leg. Marie can finally read its collar: "Bea." The cat recognizes her name and replies by purring. After Marie brushes dirt from its white fur, the cat leads her out of the bushes and into an opening.

They emerge at the opposite side from where Marie entered. There is in fact a lawn behind the overgrowth and vegetation. And a house that looks unlike the other houses on Maplewood Drive. There are two stories of dark gray wood, and pockets of moss seep through the paneling. No wonder Marie couldn't see it from the street. The house is well camouflaged. It must have been here before the other houses were built, a remnant of a neighborhood that came before the suburban developers. Bea scampers onto the porch. If she belongs to anyone nearby, they must have lived in this house. So Marie follows the cat to the door. She can feel the floorboards bend beneath her feet on her way there, though the cat doesn't seem to mind. Marie half expects Freddy Kreuger to answer the door before she even reaches the doorbell. The cat meows against the door to confirm that this is where she belongs. Marie rings the doorbell.

Nothing.

The cat stops meowing and stands in place, her eyes glued to the door patiently waiting for whoever might answer it.

Marie rings the bell again. This time she can hear someone shuffling from the inside. She can also feel the floor bend as the footsteps come closer. Slowly but surely, whoever is coming reaches the other side of the door. Marie wonders if the floor can support both their weight, plus Bea who is still eagerly waiting for the door to open. She had already crawled her way out of thorns and branches. There is no way she would crawl out of a hole from a stranger's porch.

"Excuse me," Marie says, hoping the person can hear her. "I found your cat—Bea? She was caught in some thorns over there."

Again, the cat meows at the sound of her name. The person inside seems to be reassured by her meow, too, because now the deadbolt lock turns, and then the doorknob turns as well.

"Kamusta," the woman says. She is not who Marie expected, far from the Freddy Krueger type. She is an elderly Filipino woman with long white hair—almost as white as Bea's white fur coat. She is also wearing a white gown. Not a fancy kind of gown, but the kind Marie's mother wears at night to go to bed. A loose shirt that runs down the length of the body. She continues to speak in Tagalog, "I'm sorry for my appearance. I wasn't expecting anyone at this time." She bends down towards Bea, who gladly receives the woman's pets.

Marie tries to remember if she knows this woman. She met many old Filipino women at church, or whenever her mother hosted Friday night rosary at their house. She never memorized their names. She and Anna would normally hang out with the other girls their age. At church, they had their youth group, but they would be too busy on their phones or gossiping with each other about what happened in the past week of school to focus on the message of the gospel. When the women came over for rosary, Anna would go to Sarah's house and that's when their mother made Marie go too. But this woman in front of her must be part of her mother's Catholic "support group." All the Filipinos in the neighborhood know each other.

"Thank you," the woman says. "I am old and beginning to forget things. Luckily, Bea is forgiving. Forget then forgive—isn't that right, Bea?" The cat purrs, still happy to be reunited with her owner. The woman looks up at Marie. "You look like you've seen a ghost."

Marie realizes she hasn't spoken a word.

"Um," she starts. "I didn't think a Filipino woman would live here."

"You wouldn't be the first to think that," the woman says. "My name is Lucia. Why don't you come inside and I can tell you all about myself?" *This is how every horror movie starts*, Marie thinks. "At least have a cup of coffee and a slice of leche flan as a thank you for saving Bea."

As if to contribute to the woman's invitation, Bea begins to wrap herself around Marie's legs, purring, whining, and walking in an infinity loop to trap her. The cat is convincing. With still a few hours to kill before she has to pick up Anna, Marie makes up her mind to stay for a while. Besides, if Lucia is more dangerous than she looks, Marie can easily free herself from the old woman. But she doubts she'll have to resort to such extreme measures.

★

While Lucia prepares the coffee and flan, Marie takes in the interior of the house. If the outside seemed out of place, the inside is all the more strange. Rather than the bright, egg-white painted walls and beige carpeted floors of her own house, everything is hardwood; everything is stained in brown. From the paneling all over the corners of the walls to the floors that seem not to reflect light but darkness. The heavy burgundy curtains are drawn closed, and the room is lit by the dim orange hue of a chandelier. Over the mantelpiece are some framed pictures in black and white, but Marie is seated too far to make them out. How old is this house exactly? Marie begins to regret her decision to come inside, but before she can make another move, Lucia enters and sets down a cup and plate in front of Marie. She made two cups of instant coffee without any milk or sugar. She explains that the leche flan has all the milk and sugar they'll need, so it is better to pair the dessert with black coffee. Marie doesn't complain, even though she hates black coffee. She takes a bite of flan, which is quite good. She takes a sip of the coffee, and despite it being instant coffee, it does pair well with the flan.

"I might have seen you at church," Marie says to break the ice in between mouthfuls. Marie needs the reassurance more than Lucia, who is seated in a chair across from Marie and has Bea sitting on her lap. Meanwhile, Marie sits stiffly on a couch with a plastic seat cover over it. Any slight move makes a squeaking sound, and Marie would like to make this scene the least awkward as possible. "You might know my mother. She knows everyone at church."

"Oh, no. I haven't been to church in a long time," she says. "Not since my husband's funeral."

"I'm sorry," Marie says, feeling guilty for having reminded her.

"Don't be. That was a very long time ago."

When Lucia stands up from her chair, the cat jumps off her lap and scurries over to Marie. The woman walks to the fireplace and eyes some of the photos on the mantel. She chooses one and hands it to Marie.

"My husband and I," Lucia says. She returns to her chair. "His name was George."

Bea, now sitting on Marie's lap, appears to look at the picture too, gazing at the distant but familiar faces. There is a smiling white man in an American military uniform. He has a chiseled jaw and curly hair. Lucia's skin is smooth, and her hair is a deep black, contrary to the wintry white hair she has now. She is also smiling. Behind them is a familiar backdrop, one Marie visited on numerous field trips as a child. A tall obelisk pierces the sky, and in front is the statue of José Rizal, a copy of *Noli Me Tángere* in his hand. "This is in Manila," Marie says.

"Yes, 1945," Lucia says. "I was nineteen in that picture. George was twenty-three. He and the other Americans helped end the war." Marie attempts some quick mental math to calculate how old the woman in front of her is now. *Old,* she estimates, *really old.*

"I was a nurse in one of the barracks. I was tending to him. If you look closely, you can see he's still standing on a limp." Marie thought the man merely had an arm around Lucia, but now she notices that he is using her for support. "He thought the best way to repay me was with a hand in marriage. I was nineteen and naive, and he promised me a good life in the States. So I said yes, and we were married not even a month after the war ended." Lucia pauses mid-thought, then takes a breath. Was it nostalgia or regret?

"I left behind my parents and my sister," Lucia says. "It was an exciting time for the Philippines then. Murmurings of independence. The country was becoming a country. The Americans were finally leaving, and the people of the Philippines would be free to rule themselves. My sister was thirteen then, so she stayed with my parents in Manila. Had I known I would not see them again, I may not have been so eager to marry George. My sister is the one who took that picture. Beatrice."

Marie tries to conjure an image of what Lucia's sister may have looked like behind the camera, if Beatrice was just as happy as Lucia and George. She and her own sister share similar enough features—the same dark brown eyes, long black hair, and button nose. The difference between Marie and Anna is in their face shape: Anna's is slender like their father's, and Marie's is round like their mother's. If Lucia was nineteen and Beatrice was thirteen, the similarities might have been as distant as their ages. And if Lucia hasn't seen her sister since 1945, Beatrice might look drastically different from what she remembers. Lucia surely wouldn't recognize her now. But thinking about Lucia and her sister leads Marie to another thought: Bea the cat, who is curled up around herself, purring. Marie strokes her white fur.

"You named the cat after your sister?" she asks.

"It's a strange thing to do, isn't it?"

"No, no. I didn't mean it like that." Marie does think it strange. Nothing in the world could make her name a pet after Anna. She wouldn't dare reincarnate her sister into an animal just to live with the daily reminder of how selfish and snobbish Anna has been. She wouldn't dare curse an animal with her sister's name. Afraid that she may have offended Lucia, Marie tells Lucia about her own sister.

"I also have a younger sister. Her name is Anna. She is thirteen."

"The same age as Beatrice when I left," Lucia points out. "You must be a great Ate for looking after her. For staying with her."

My parents didn't really give me a choice, Marie wanted to say. Instead, she says, "My family moved into the neighborhood a few months ago."

"You came as a family. That's good." Marie could see the lament on Lucia's face. After a pause, Lucia decides to return to her story. "When George and I moved into the neighborhood, it was all very different. A different time, even a different place. Many people were moving to the suburbs. Of course, none of them were Filipino. For many years, I was the only one. George used much of his inheritance to commission this house. It's in the same condition as it was back then. No renovations, even after the suburban developers tried paying me for it, or to at least remodel it after their own design. George wouldn't have wanted that."

For a moment, the floor upstairs creeks. Only Marie notices. Is her husband really dead?

Bea is comfortably seated on her lap, still purring, while Lucia continues her story.

"I kept in touch with my family in those early years. Beatrice and I wrote letters back and forth. She told me about every boyfriend and every breakup, and how she eventually went to college to become a journalist. I was so proud of her when she finally grew up to become a fine young woman and a reporter at *The Manila Gazette.*"

"You didn't want to visit?" Marie asks, wondering what kept Lucia from returning home to the people she missed.

"I don't know why really." Lucia pauses, then admits, "Pride. I didn't want my parents to think I regretted my decision. I wanted to show them that George was the right man, and that settling in the States was the right decision. I was happy, relatively. George still had some of his inheritance left, and he worked at the power plant. We lived comfortably. I told myself I would endure this life, even if it was a bit lonely.

"By the time I wanted to go back, it was too late. It was sometime in the early seventies when Beatrice sent me letters warning about what was to come in the Philippines. 'Corruption,' she wrote, 'Corruption at the highest level.' Then the President declared martial law. I begged her and my parents to join me here. We had plenty of room in this house, and George would welcome them, I promised her. But our parents were already old, she argued, and there was no life for them in America. I said I would visit them instead. She said it was no longer safe in the Philippines. Then silence. Her letters stopped coming. It took some time before I finally realized there would be nothing left for me to return to."

Marie knows all too well what happened. Ferdinand Marcos seized power and targeted people like Beatrice, reporters and journalists who sought to undermine him. Beatrice and her parents must have been a few of the casualties. Who knows what happened to them, either silenced on the spot or taken to one of the military camps to be tortured?

"I used to think that maybe one of these days, Beatrice would come moving into the neighborhood too. That one day I'd be at the grocery store and bump into her. She'd be married, maybe with children. George and I would invite them over for dinner. And we would relive the missing years we spent apart. But that reunion never came. When a stray cat made its way into the neighborhood a couple of years ago, no one else would take care of her. So I did. I named her Bea after my sister. Pathetic, I know."

"I'm sorry that happened to you," is all Marie can find the words to say.

"No point worrying over it now," Lucia says coldly. She pauses, perhaps taking in all the things she had hidden for so long. "How's the leche flan, by the way?"

"It was really good," she says. Marie didn't realize she had finished eating her flan. Her cup of coffee, too, is empty. She checks the time and realizes she's been in the house for two and a half hours. It can't have been that long, can it?

"I still have some of mine left." The old woman points out the slice of flan on her plate; she hadn't taken a bite. This worries Marie. Why wouldn't Lucia eat her own flan? But there wasn't anything nefarious baked into the flan, Marie assures herself. It tasted, as it should, like sugar. No way she would tell her sister or mother about this. She is the older sibling—she should have known better.

"Bea," Lucia calls the cat, waking her. "Come get some." After a brief stretch and yawn, Bea follows her orders, leaping from Marie's lap onto the plate of flan Lucia sets on the floor. The cat immediately buries her mouth in it.

"Are you sure she should be eating that?"

"Don't be silly. This was Beatrice's favorite dessert when we were growing up. And I made it from my mother's recipe." Strange. Naming a cat after your long-lost sister is one thing, but feeding a cat as if she were your sister is another. She remembers how old Lucia must be, at least ninety. Surely, at her age, some common sense has lapsed. But from all appearances, Lucia is fully healthy and capable. After all, she lives alone in this two-story house—unless, of course, she isn't alone. Marie doesn't want to stay long enough to find out.

"I better get going," Marie says as she stands up from the couch, puts on her backpack, and motions for the door. "I have to pick up my sister from a friend's house and I'm already late."

"Already? Why not take some slices for your sister and family."

"No, it's alright, really. But thank you."

"You are welcome any time," Lucia says as she walks Marie to the door. "Bring your sister next time."

"It was nice meeting you." Marie doubts she will take the invitation in the future.

Outside it is dark. Marie can already hear her mother's nagging voice, reprimanding her for keeping Anna out so late. She picks up her pace and doesn't look back. She sprints through the bushes, the same ones where she found Bea, and finds her way back to Maplewood Drive. She focuses on the walk to Sarah's house, trying to forget the faint sound of Lucia murmuring, like a purring, as she closed the door behind her.

★

Her mother hadn't heard of any woman named Lucia, not from church nor the neighborhood in general. Marie told her mother and sister that she was at the public library all evening. She spent the rest of that night awake in bed, partially from the instant coffee she'd had at Lucia's, partially from the fear and wonder of the whole experience. If Lucia had truly lived alone, then what made the floors creak upstairs? If she accepted losing her sister in the Philippines, why treat her cat as if her sister were still alive? She can't tell anyone about her strange, strange night with the elderly Filipino woman and her cat. In the next few days, she avoids the house at the end of Maplewood Drive at all costs.

That is until Halloween night. Marie and Anna have to take the boys, Angelo and Daniel, trick-or-treating. The boys are dressed as Mario and Luigi. Marie threw together a Darna costume, just as she planned—though it's mostly a slightly altered Wonder Woman costume she found at Party City. Anna wears a preppy 80s outfit to emulate Nancy Thompson: a pink sweater vest and khaki pants. She makes sure to add some red food coloring in a few spots to emulate blood. Although Marie had insisted that they go with just the boys to trick-or-treat, Anna invited Kevin and Sarah to join them. "I need Kevin to match my costume. Otherwise, it's pointless," Anna had argued. Kevin, of course, was Freddy Kreuger, wearing a green and red striped sweater and a fedora. Sarah was in all black, like Allison from *The Breakfast Club* before the makeover at the end of the movie that took away what made her so cool.

Once they finish asking for candy on Maplewood Drive, the eclectic group of pop-culture-inspired trick-or-treaters finally reach the end of the street. They've knocked on every door, except for Lucia's. Surprisingly, all the shrubbery has been cut down and mowed. The yard is as open as every other yard in the neighborhood. The house, however, remains. Its two stories of dark gray wood are no longer covered in moss; it seems to have been washed. One key difference from the last time Marie was there is the For Sale sign planted in front of it.

"One more house," the boys say, pulling Marie and Anna towards it.

But Marie wants nothing more than to turn around.

"No one lives there. It's for sale," Marie says. "And you have enough candy," she adds.

"First one to ring the doorbell gets all my candy," Kevin screams, already sprinting across the lawn.

"Hey, stop!" Marie is more desperate and serious now. "It isn't safe."

"Oh, come on," Anna says. "You're being paranoid. It's just like any other house." Anna takes Angelo and Daniel by the hand and leads them straight to the front door. Sarah is right behind them.

There would be no harm, Marie tells herself. No matter how strange Lucia was the other night, Marie left perfectly unharmed. "Wait for me," she finally says, talking herself out of her fear.

One of the boys rings the doorbell.

Nothing.

The other boy rings it again. "Trick or treat," he says. Again, there is nothing. Not any shuffling from inside the house, not the creaking floorboards like last time, not even a meow from a cat.

"I told you there was no one here," Marie says with relief. "Let's go home."

After Kevin knocks on the door with his makeshift cardboard claws and receives yet another blank response, the group begins to walk back to the street.

"Look," one of the boys says. He is pointing to a window on the second floor. It is dimly lit from the inside, as if by candlelight. Seated on the windowsill isn't a jack-o-lantern, like every other house on Maplewood Drive. Instead, sitting on the ledge are two small creatures that could be nothing else but cats, their triangle ears distinctly facing outward. Two pairs of glowing, yellow eyes are staring down at them, though Marie feels their concentration on her. Because she knows these cats. She knows this pair of lost souls in their second or third lives. Lucia and Bea, light and beauty, with their fur as white as bone.

DRESS DOWN DAY

In the second grade, the Catholic school had us bring home manila envelopes each week, full of notices and forms for the parents to peruse. The specific flyer Mama held in her hands was for an upcoming "dress down day," a day when students were excused from wearing school uniforms. I had no care for the clothes—a white button-down, black necktie, and khakis. But I dreaded the shoes. I can still feel my feet resisting their own bend after years in those black leather Oxfords, which held my toes in tight like a bundle of stems in a ceramic vase.

"Wear red, white, *and* blue," Mama said, reading the flyer aloud. "Does that mean all of them at once or separately?"

"We paid for his uniform," Papa said. "Now we're paying again for him *not* to wear it?"

"It's for Veterans Day," Mama explained. "And it's only a dollar."

"Veterans Day?" Papa said, continuing his tirade. "We're paying tuition. And where does the church collection go? We already do our share of charity work."

"It's only a dollar, Ronaldo," she insisted. "Heck, I paid a dollar for him to wear his Halloween costume last week. Did you want him to be the only one without a costume then?" She had bought me a ninja costume from the dollar store, a black jumpsuit and bandana made of thin fabric, which, for some reason, had glitter all over it. I wanted to be the Blue Power Ranger, but Mama decided thirty dollars at Party City wasn't worth one day of dressing down in a costume I'd never wear again. Being a ninja for a day was good enough.

"Well, now we've given them two extra dollars two weeks in a row." Papa walked out of the living room and into the bedroom. "We're not rich," he said under his breath.

"Red, white, and blue," Mama said to herself, giving up on her husband who offered no useful input. She turned her attention to me, a seven-year-old boy in overalls. "Did they say anything else at school? Does it matter which color exactly?"

I shrugged.

"I'm sure we can find something."

She began rummaging through the closet in the living room. I kept all my clothes there in plastic bins and cardboard boxes. We didn't sort much of our things when we first moved into the apartment. After all, the apartment was small and there wasn't a lot of room for things to go into anyway. Most of them were clothes with faded colors, shirts and shorts that I owned even before we immigrated to the States. Basketball jerseys with misprinted numbers of famous NBA players, polo shirts with logos that resembled higher-end brands but were slightly tilted or curved at odd ends—imperfect clothing for those who couldn't afford fashion, but close enough that they could have easily fooled at a glance. My dollar store ninja costume reemerged, only to be thrown carelessly onto the floor.

"We should send some of these back home to your cousins." Then Mama clapped her hands together in a moment of epiphany.

She tossed out some more clothes onto the floor, over the sofa, and some even on me, moving other plastic bins out of the way. "Grab me a chair," she told me, and I followed. I placed it in front of her so she could climb it. Then she reached toward the top compartment, moving her arm into a mystery box like a magician into her top hat. But when she finally pulled back her hand, there wasn't a rabbit. Instead, Mama had retrieved another off-brand polo shirt, but this one was the specific shirt she had in mind.

"What's all that noise," Papa said, returning from the bedroom. "And what the hell is all this doing on the floor?"

"Look, Ronaldo," Mama said, spreading out the shirt to show him and me. "It was Lola's going-away present for Marcillo when we first left."

It was exactly what the flyer asked for—red, white, and blue altogether. Each color had a row layered on top of one another. A logo was stitched just under one of the polo's lapels: a golden sun with three rays spreading out from its curves. It was clearly a shirt meant to represent the Philippines, its own flag the same red, white, and blue with a golden sun.

"All this mess for a shirt?" Papa said. He looked at me with disappointed eyes, eyes that had just woken up from a nap, eyes that crucified me onto the floor. "You help your mother with *that*." He pointed out the scattered piles of clothes throughout the living room.

I nodded, obedient like a dog.

He continued to the kitchen where he fetched himself a bottle of beer from the refrigerator.

"Come here," Mama said to me. "Let's see if it still fits." She lifted the shirt open for me so I can slip my head through it. It was a little snug, my seven-year-old baby fat proudly protruding. Still, Mama said, "Perfect fit!"

"That's not American enough." Papa sipped his beer.

"What do you mean not American enough?" Mama replied. "It's red, white, and blue, isn't it?"

"Those veterans didn't die for you."

"We fought alongside the Americans."

"But we are *not* Americans," Papa declared.

"Marcillo's got every right to wear this shirt to school," Mama said, brushing away specks of dust up and down my shirt. "We'll iron it out and you'll fit right in with the rest of them."

Papa had already finished his first beer when he reached into the fridge for another. Before he retreated into the bedroom again, he said, "A dollar to be American for a day. How I wish."

Mama was right, though. On Veterans Day at school, I wore the polo, even though the Philippine sun marked it. I couldn't help but feel too formal compared to the others. They merely wore T-shirts with American flags or bald eagles. But it didn't matter if we wore all three colors at once or a selection of any one of them. We all eventually blended into each other, hands against hearts as we recited the morning pledge of allegiance in the auditorium. That my shirt represented an entirely different country never crossed anyone's mind. "A dollar to be American for a day," Papa had said.

★

Years later, when Papa's liver could no longer catch up to the bottles in the fridge, the day eventually came when we were to take our citizenship test without him. It was July, a slathering of heat against the skin. But even as the sweat started seeping through my pores as I stepped out of the shower, Mama peeped her head into my room to remind me, "Wear red, white, and blue. And a nice pair of khakis." Even in late adolescence, I was still her boy, whom she dressed up to fit her ideal image of an American son. There was no arguing with her demands. Mama knew best.

I opened my closet to find everything I owned was blue, black, and gray. Blue was still my favorite color. But Mama said to wear something more patriotic. It was, after all, the day of our citizenship test, and that meant more to her than it did to me. When Papa died, she had doubled her efforts to become American. She invested in a proper immigration lawyer by working odd jobs, from babysitting to dishwashing, before finally landing a stable job at my same childhood Catholic school serving lunch meals to the children.

"Make sure you iron your clothes, too," Mama said, poking her head in again. "We're going to take pictures after."

I owned nothing red, and the original Veterans Day polo with the Philippine sun had already been shipped back to the Philippines in a cardboard box years ago. So I picked out a plaid blue and white shirt, a pair of khakis that had belonged to Papa that I had grown into, then took the time to iron my outfit.

I looked at myself in the mirror when I finished and saw his reflection. I was seventeen, but my father's features had already made their way to the surface. I paused at his haunting, the man who ran away from his homeland but never from his vices. He embraced the liquor bottles wherever he went and took me and Mama along with him. Even after his death, he continued to embrace me, his face masking mine somewhere lost beneath.

I wanted to tell him how Mama and I made it without him. I wanted to tell him how it costs more than a dollar to be American, more than the years waited and forms signed and dated, more than the questions about the government's three branches, more than some simple written English test I could have passed when I was seven and he was still alive.

Papa somehow knew that there was no difference between that cheap Halloween costume and the polo shirt that barely fit. Since then, I spent a decade putting on other costumes, parroting patriotism, as if I were just like everyone else. But Papa saw through it all back then, and now so do I. I wanted to tell him that wearing red, white, and blue wouldn't have made any difference at all—not to them, but most of all, not to me—that he was right to say, "That's not American enough." No holiday, no dress down day, could have made me feel patriotic. When my passport came in the mail weeks later, I felt no such change.

But all that was still ahead of me. The test was a few hours away.

"Ready?" Mama said. She, of course, had bought her outfit weeks prior. She began planning as soon as the interview date was set. She wore a long, striped dress—three stripes of red, white, and blue—which flowed freely down her torso to her waist, then was pleated from there to her knees, so that when she spun around, her dress blossomed into an American spiral.

Then out the door we went, Mama and me, to become citizens.

A BRIEF STINT AT THE FAIRLEIGHS'

She would prove them wrong, Mrs. Bautista thought. She would prove her husband and son wrong. She found motivation in the thinking of it. After all, it was Mr. Bautista who brought her from the Philippines to the States and convinced her of opportunity. And now that she's found one, why couldn't he find it in himself to support her? She was looking to fill the absence left by her son Mark, and working beyond the walls of their one-less-person home would be her escape from its negative space.

"Family seeks a housemaid who can cook, clean, and babysit during the day," she read from the flyer to her husband, a high school teacher in the city.

"You already do that here, for us," he said.

Mark had left to work at a startup company earlier in the summer. Something to do with microchips and self-service kiosks, just some of the things Mrs. Bautista never understood about her son. When he decided to leave in May despite not needing to be there until August, she protested. "I have to adjust," Mark reasoned. "I can't just go from New Jersey to California cold turkey."

Cold turkey, she repeated in her head. Who taught him that phrase? What that meant for Mrs. Bautista was that she, too, would have to adjust without Mark, *cold turkey*. She had wanted to spend one last summer with him in the house. She worked as a teacher's aide in the local middle school, and she usually continued through the summer for some extra money. But she intentionally passed up the opportunity this summer— Mark's last summer before he went off to the West Coast. His decision to move so early caught her off guard.

"I took the summer off for you," she argued. With every shrug of his shoulder, with every unabashed "Whatever," she felt a tearing at her heart. After she and Mr. Bautista dropped their son off at the airport, an unceremonious occasion, Mrs. Bautista was left home alone most of her days.

"You'll cook and clean for someone else," Mr. Bautista continued. "Back home, we had our own katulong to do all those things."

"Then why did we leave?" she rebutted, and with that she won and had her way. *For us*, Mr. Bautista wanted to say, but they both knew they had moved because of him and him alone.

Had she not cooked and cleaned for someone other than herself, looked after their son, bathed him, helped him with his homework while her husband taught other parents' children, brought up Mark through his adolescent rage—only for him to go away after college, without a second thought? She was qualified to be a katulong now more than ever, and she needed—wanted—to fill her time rather than sullenly page through cooking and home improvement channels all summer. Besides, the salary was good and with enough saved, they could finally pay off the house, which was meant for the three of them, but now, just the two.

"Mark left us, Eduardo," Mrs. Bautista said after their little debate.

"He's his own man now. Even you have to let him be." Her husband seemed to take their son's departure more lightly. Although he didn't openly encourage Mark to leave, he made no effort to dissuade him. "If he thinks it's the best for his career, why shouldn't he go?" he said.

"He should have gotten a job closer to us," Mrs. Bautista said back.

"What's done is done."

Mrs. Bautista, feeling outnumbered, alone in her hold over her son, shied away from arguing anymore.

She merely said, "Can you at least drop me off at the bus stop tomorrow?"

★

Mr. Bautista dropped her off before his own morning commute into the city. Mrs. Bautista took a forty-five-minute bus ride north, then walked up a hill before finally reaching the Fairleighs' front door. Now in her late forties, she was no longer the young woman who held onto her four-year-old son from Manila to Newark to meet her husband at the airport. "Made in Manila," she had teased Mark when he got older, "The Philippines' greatest export!" Now her son had grown to walk on his own, beyond her arm's reach, and gravity took its toll on her. She felt the weight of each step as she walked up the hill. She would bring two pairs of shoes next time, she noted, flats for work and sneakers for the climb.

The Fairleigh house was beyond the size of her home—hers, despite being a two-story house, was the smallest on the block, while theirs was a triptych Greek revival, a mansion with flourished Corinthian columns. She had seen houses like these on television—their owners always looking to refurbish a wide-open kitchen, or some new homeowners with outrageous budgets scouting them in open houses. Now, tired and out of breath, she reached the foot of the Fairleighs' driveway and panted.

There was a jet-black luxury Chrysler and a bleeding red Mercedes-Benz. She took out her phone and thought of sending a picture to her husband. How bongga was her new job, and her employers, she would brag to her husband later. As she took a number of pictures—zooming in and out of the columns and the frieze over the door, an intricate stone weaving of sculpted foliage—a tall, squarish man opened the door and walked outside towards her.

"Shet," she cursed under her breath, fumbling her phone back into her purse. *Idiot: you're going to ruin this for yourself and prove them right!*

"You must be Elena." The man reached out a greeting hand. "I'm Stephen Fairleigh." He said her name like a fairytale character, Eh-LAY-na. She had always pronounced her name with her mother tongue, Eh-leh-NA, but she wouldn't dare correct her new employer, intimidating all on his own. Mr. Fairleigh was built like a box, bulky and staunch but not as sculpted as a boxer—angular rather than muscular. He was bald on top, but had a white beard growing in, a striking, snowcapped jaw.

"Yes," Mrs. Bautista said, "nice to meet you, Sir." She shook his hand, flustered. "I was only making sure this was the right house," she tried to explain, covering for the impromptu photo op on her phone. His grip was stable enough, so perhaps he didn't notice her trembling. Her nerves moved elsewhere, rattling the delicate bones supporting her legs—the climb up the hill had already

71

weakened them. She quickly took her hand back. She reached for a handkerchief in her purse, wiped the sweat from her forehead, and rearranged her hair. She apologized for her appearance.

"Oh, no need for that. We're glad you made it out here so promptly." The job ad had only been posted in the local paper for a week.

"It was no problem, Sir." Mrs. Bautista knew to address such authority figures with the titles of Sir or Ma'am, the way the store clerks in Filipino shopping malls greeted every customer. Of course, she had found it annoying when they hounded her as Ma'am when all she wanted to do was look around at a few dresses. But she knew it was part of the job, that getting caught without offering any overt hospitality would lead them right to a talking-to from their boss. She made sure to leave a better first impression on Mr. Fairleigh. "Your home is so beautiful."

"Isn't she?" He smiled, eyeing the mansion left and right. Hopefully some of its beauty would rub off on her, Mrs. Bautista thought. "Come on, let me show you inside."

"Yes, sir." She recovered herself and, taking a deep breath, followed after him.

★

"Rachel," Mr. Fairleigh called over a woman hunched over an iPad on the marble countertop. He stepped aside to let Mrs. Bautista, a mere chess piece—a pawn—into view. "This is Elena. She'll be working for us."

"Hi, Ma'am," she muttered sheepishly to Mrs. Fairleigh. "It's a pleasure to meet you."

"How kind," she replied. "And please, call me Rachel."

"Sorry, M— I mean, Rachel."

"That's better," Mrs. Fairleigh said with firm approval. She was younger than her husband and reminded Mrs. Bautista of Olivia Newton-John. She embodied both prim-and-proper Sandy and her greaser alter-ego, a fine line between book club and dance club. She was the American woman Mrs. Bautista knew from the American movies she watched as a child in Manila. She had aspired to be Marilyn Monroe and Katherine Hepburn—an ambitious little brown girl could imagine. Surely, Mrs. Fairleigh didn't need to imagine much at all.

"I don't know, hun," Mr. Fairleigh interrupted. "'Sir'…I like the ring to it."

"Don't let it get to your head," his wife said. "Call him whatever you want, Elena." She winked.

"Alright, before we get too comfortable, let's talk about why you're here." Stephen Fairleigh redirected his attention to Mrs. Bautista. "Rachel recently started her own business venture."

Mrs. Fairleigh lifted her iPad for Mrs. Bautista to see. She swiped one image after another, a series of intricate outfits shown in spotlight. "These were all taken just upstairs, in my bedroom," Mrs. Fairleigh explained. "All made by me. I've only just started pursuing my dream in fashion."

"A very expensive dream," her husband added.

Some of us don't have the luxury of big-tech husbands to pursue our own dreams, Mrs. Bautista wanted to say.

Mr. Fairleigh continued. "Which is why we need a little help around the house. C'mon, let me show you around."

Mrs. Bautista followed, staring in awe at the mansion. Such a big house for a three-person family. She, Mr. Bautista, and Mark all managed with a little two-bedroom, one bath. Mark's room had been upstairs. Once he became a teenager, there were days when she never got to see him; either he never left his room, or by the time he did come home from a night out with friends it was already past midnight. Maybe his moving away didn't make much difference after all. But here at the Fairleighs', every room seemed too big for just one person. Even Mrs. Fairleigh had a separate room from her husband with a private office where she could work. There was even a view of the lake from their backyard.

"Wow," Mrs. Bautista couldn't help saying when he led her outside.

"One of the perks of living on top of the hill," Mr. Fairleigh admitted. He diverted his attention elsewhere. "Gar!" he called out, searching. "He loves playing hide and seek. Gar!"

From their backyard playground, a little boy came running. Gareth Fairleigh tilted his head with a curious urgency, looking up at Mrs. Bautista. "He's eight years old," Mr. Fairleigh explained, "and he's starting the third grade in the fall, isn't that right, Gar?" The boy nodded nervously, his long blonde hair brushing against his plump cheeks. He was wearing overalls, which reminded Mrs. Bautista of her own son when he was his age. "This is Miss Elena. She'll be taking care of you while Mommy begins working."

"Nice to meet you," Elena said, bending to his height, reaching out her hand. Gar looked up at his father first, for permission, before returning the greeting. After their brief handshake, the little boy sprinted away, back into his own playground world.

"That's our Gareth," Mr. Fairleigh said. "Gar, we call him." He led her back into the house.

In the kitchen, Mrs. Fairleigh was in the middle of a phone call. "You're the event coordinator—coordinate! Oh—" She turned to see that they had returned from the tour. "I have to go, but remember what your job is before I find someone else to do it for you." She hung up the phone.

"Don't worry," Mr. Fairleigh assured Mrs. Bautista. "She'll be busy at work during the week. You won't be hearing much from her then."

"I heard that," said Mrs. Fairleigh. "Before I forget: Gar has a very sensitive stomach, so his meals have been prepared in advance." She motioned for Mrs. Bautista to join her by the fridge, which was unlike any fridge Mrs. Bautista had seen before. It had no handles; instead, with just one pass of a hand, the stainless-steel panels opened up for Mrs. Fairleigh, automatic and obedient. Inside were more compartments than Mrs. Bautista could count. The middle section had a stack of trays wrapped in foil and plastic, which Mrs. Fairleigh explained were reserved for Gar. "We get these meals specially delivered for him. They're ready to heat in the microwave, so we don't expect you to cook for him. If he ever tries to convince you otherwise, don't let him eat anything else. Is that understood?"

"Yes, Ms. Rachel."

"Just *Rachel*." She continued to show Mrs. Bautista the other compartments. There were varieties of vegetables, meats, dressings, and sauces. Both side panels were crowded with juices, milks, and a few beers. "These are all fresh and organic ingredients," Mrs. Fairleigh explained. "Aside from Gar's food, feel free to take some when you need. You can surely cook for yourself."

"Yes, thank you," Mrs. Bautista said. "Thank you, *Rachel*."

"Great! I think that's everything. Do your job well and you won't hear a peep from me."

"As you can tell, my wife has a very blunt way of putting things," Mr. Fairleigh said as he led her back out. He made sure his wife was out of sight. "She can seem like a control freak, but she's harmless. Truthfully, we're both excited to have you with us. We'll see you on Monday."

"Yes, sir," Mrs. Bautista said.

"I could really get used to that," Mr. Fairleigh said to himself as he closed the door. "*Sir.*"

★

Mrs. Bautista started that Monday. For the most part, she stuck to her chores vehemently. She arrived early in the morning, calculating the extra minutes it would take to climb the hill from the bus stop to their house—and she brought an extra pair of sneakers, which she quickly changed out of before arriving at the doorstep.

"Remember," Mr. Bautista had warned, "you work for them. Don't be fooled by their kindness." She kept her husband's words in the back of her mind.

Mr. and Mrs. Fairleigh were indeed nice. Though she only saw Mr. Fairleigh at the beginning and end of her shift, as he would go into the city to run his company as CEO. Mrs. Bautista didn't know much about it, only that— in Mr. Fairleigh's words—"The company is the biggest supplier of algorithmic software on the East Coast." It sounded impressive. If she did her job right, Mrs. Bautista could ask Mr. Fairleigh if there was a place for her son there. The company would be a step-up from wherever Mark was in California, and it would bring him closer to home.

At the same time, Mrs. Fairleigh went with her husband into the city, designing new clothes and coordinating with the rest of her team in her new fashion headquarters in SoHo. However, there was one instance when Mrs. Bautista spoke with Mrs. Fairleigh just before they left for the city.

"You're Filipino, aren't you? Did I guess right?" she asked.

"Yes," Mrs. Bautista responded. "I am Filipino."

"Do you know about Gianni Versace?"

Of course Mrs. Bautista knew. There were Versace stores in the malls of Manila, but the brand name was rampant among street vendors, along with Gucci and Lacoste, names and brands she would only own as stitched-on logos on lesser fabrics. She nodded.

Mrs. Fairleigh continued, "It was a Filipino who killed him. Tragic. Iconic."

Did she mean *ironic*? Mrs. Bautista didn't know what to make of it. She found comfort in the thought that her employer was simply trying to make conversation.

When she later told her husband about their exchange, Mr. Bautista supposed it was "A test of wit," the way his students taunted him by calling him Jackie Chan on the first day of school. "She wants you to know she's in control." Rachel, not Ma'am, Mrs. Bautista reminded herself.

Fortunately, Mr. Fairleigh was right. She didn't hear much more from Rachel Fairleigh after they left for the city. Instead, Mrs. Bautista spent most of the summer with the Fairleighs' son. During her first few days at the mansion, Gar was quiet. "Good morning, Gar," Mrs. Bautista said when she arrived. But each time she approached him, the boy retreated into another room of the house. His parents' absence made the Fairleigh home bigger, an effect Mrs. Bautista knew all too well. If she were to win her employers' favor, she would first need to win over Gar. She knew that the one thing a child craves more than anything is attention. Sooner or later, the wall between her and Gar would crumble.

It was the same hope she had for her and her own son. She knew it would take time, that her son would reach out eventually. They still hadn't spoken in the weeks after he left. He chose to be "his own man" in California, despite the fact that she had given up her summer to be with him. Mrs. Bautista would wait for her son to apologize.

In the meantime, there was always something new to clean at the Fairleighs'. Gar's scattered toys throughout the house, along with the usual cleaning and laundry. With that much surface area, there was plenty for dust to cling to.

School was still months away. But Gar was a curious child with an impulse to learn, as Mrs. Bautista found, and his inquisitive eight-year-old mind eventually warmed up to her.

"Manila is the capital of the Philippines." He spoke up suddenly. It had been some weeks after she started.

"What?" Mrs. Bautista turned off the vacuum, surprised to hear the boy speak.

"That's where you live," the boy said. He pointed to a book in his lap. "It says here, 'Manila is the capital of the Philippines.'"

"I don't live there anymore, but I used to," she explained. She left the vacuum and joined Gar on the couch. She read the title of the book, *World Capitals: A Global Picture Book*. On the page were pictures of a farmer and his carabao, an Igorot boy wearing a loincloth, a bahay kubo on a beach— one wouldn't find such scenes in the capital city. "But, yes, Manila is the capital of the Philippines."

"What's it like there?"

"Hmm." Mrs. Bautista paused to think about where to start. She reminisced about their home, a pastel painted house in one of Manila's outer suburbs, and the traffic trying to get there, like rowing upstream; then about her parents' farm, where she spent most of her girlhood, where stray dogs flirted with cattle. She tried to describe her country simply. "The city is very crowded and full of cars, so the most beautiful things are farther away, in the countryside, in the mountains, on the beaches, where the ocean is as blue as the sky. It's either very hot and dry, or very hot and wet."

"My mom's been to a lot of these places." He turned to other pages of the book—Paris, London, Rome, Madrid. "She owns a store. She's always looking for clothes from these places to put there. But I don't think she's been to Manila."

"Well, she always wears such beautiful clothes," Mrs. Bautista said, immediately aware of her own plain clothing, a black blouse and khaki pants. When she had seen Rachel Fairleigh in the morning, the American fashionista wore a gray plaid blazer with navy blue pants, a mismatch in lesser hands, but with the correct shading and hue, Mrs. Fairleigh mastered the chaos. Though those fabrics were in Rachel Fairleigh's control, was Gar too much for her? Rachel was a young mother, but so was Mrs. Bautista when she had Mark. As far as Mrs. Bautista could tell, Gar was a saint, a reserved, docile boy with a yearning to explore.

"It's good to hear your voice, Gar." With a warm smile, Mrs. Bautista brushed Gar's blonde strands away from his face. "Is it alright if I call you Gar?"

He nodded, then returned to his book of world capitals.

★

"They're not all evil," Mrs. Bautista told her husband over dinner. "The boy is actually nice. Mabait."

"I didn't say they were evil," Mr. Bautista responded. "I just don't want them taking advantage of you. I deal with a lot of these parents who think they can bully me into giving their child an A just because—"

"What did you expect when we moved here?" She wanted to say when *you* moved here. "I'm not their slave, Eduardo. I can hold my own."

"I know. I just want you to be careful," her husband said, reiterating his best intentions.

Once in bed, Mr. Bautista changed the subject. "Mark called me today. I told him about your new job."

"What did he say?"

"*Whatever.*" Mr. Bautista imitated their son's monotonous disinterest. The edge of Mrs. Bautista's mouth curved slightly, tickled by the spot-on impression.

But her quick smile faded. "So, what did he want?"

"He needed help filling out some work forms."

"Susmaryosep," she scoffed. "'I'm an adult now,' he said, so he moved out. But now he can't fill out his own forms?"

"You should call him, Elena," Mr. Bautista urged her. "Talk to him."

"No," she said. "He's the one who left. He should call me first."

Besides, she had filled the absence another way. With Gar, she saw an opportunity—a possibility—to feel needed in a way she hadn't been for quite some time. Before falling asleep, she prayed on her guilty pleasure, a decade of Hail Marys, hoping at least the mother who lost her son to the world would understand.

★

Eventually, having given Gar a sense of her country through more expansive descriptions than his *World Capitals* book could offer, Mrs. Bautista taught the boy Tagalog words for things like water (tubig), potatoes (patatas), and chicken (manok). She was pointing out the ingredients in his everyday lunches of prepared foods, which were always the same. Mashed potatoes, grilled chicken, and steamed vegetables. She could tell that he grew tired of it, but Mrs. Bautista continued to follow Rachel Fairleigh's instructions. While Gar ate his special meals, she made use of the Fairleighs' bounty for her own lunch. She was surprised to see bok choy in the fridge—pechay, they called it in the Philippines. She also found some chuck roast among the meats and decided to cut it into cubes. She threw the beef and bok choy into a pot of boiling water and added some corn cobs and potatoes. She let the stew simmer into a broth while she finished other chores around the house. By lunch time, both their meals were ready.

"What's that?" the boy asked.

"We call this nilagang baka," Mrs. Bautista said, "stewed beef. Would you like to try some?" The words slipped right out of her mouth. But it was too late. Gar was already nodding his head, excited by the thought of eating something different. She figured she'd give him just the broth—that shouldn't cause any problems, right? What did a "sensitive stomach" even mean? She took a spoonful of the broth and blew on it to cool, like she used to do for her son. She lowered the spoon to his mouth, cupping a hand underneath to catch any spills. "Just a taste."

Gar closed his eyes as he slurped. Mrs. Bautista saw his nostrils flare up, the broth having done its job. "*Mmm*," he hummed. "I like ni-la-gang ba-ka." She knew from the look on his face that he wasn't just hungry for new food. Gar was hungry for knowledge of the world outside, longing to escape the walls of his grand home. There was only so much of it he could see from a picture book. Mrs. Bautista couldn't blame him; she understood the feeling of entrapment in her own house. And with such regimented meals, how could Gar not feel like a prisoner? Her affinity for the boy surpassed her fear of Rachel Fairleigh. So, when Gar asked, "Can you make me more Filipino food next time?", she gave in.

"I know just the thing," Mrs. Bautista assured him. She promised to cook something new the next day, to feed his wanderlust. "But it'll be our little secret. Promise?"

"I promise!"

Before she left, Mrs. Bautista took inventory of the Fairleighs' fridge, noting some ingredients she would need for the dish she had in mind. The next day at noon, Mrs. Bautista started browning some chicken thighs in a pot. In another pot was rice. "What's that?" Gar pointed to the ingredients lined up on the marble countertop. "What's that in Tagalog?"

"The ginger is luya," she said, pointing to each, "onion is sibuyas, garlic bawang, soy sauce toyo, vinegar suka." Gar repeated after her, with careful attention to each syllable. "Good, Gar," she encouraged. "But remember, you promised to keep this a secret, right?"

"Opo," he said naturally.

She was defying Mrs. Fairleigh's wishes, but Mrs. Bautista couldn't help her joy. She hadn't been this excited to cook for anyone, not since Mark was a boy. "What do you want to eat?" she had asked her son on their first night in their first apartment in the States. He was only four then, and despite her husband's explanation that there was no such thing as American adobo, Mark demanded, "Adobo!" So Mrs. Bautista acquiesced. She went to the nearest supermarket for the ingredients, and their first meal in the States was adobo.

When the chicken developed a light brown crust on both sides, she added ginger, onions, and garlic. Then she measured out equal parts soy sauce and vinegar. She tossed in some spoonfuls of sugar. Finally, she balanced the whole stew with a cup of water, diluting the salt in the soy sauce, assuaging the sour of vinegar, taming the sweetness of sugar.

Mrs. Bautista served the adobo in a bowl over rice. She watched Gar take a small spoonful into his mouth, chewing slowly and inquisitively. Then he took another spoonful, and another.

"How do you say 'delicious'?"

"Masarap," she said.

"This is masarap," he repeated, which made Mrs. Bautista smile, almost blushing, knowing that she had passed a test of her and her cooking, that the absence inside her was filled.

"You know, I used to cook this for my son," she said. "This was his favorite dish."

"Why doesn't he like it anymore?" he asked.

"He grew up," she answered simply.

The doorbell interrupted them, which concerned Mrs. Bautista. Mrs. Fairleigh didn't normally come home until the evening. She left Gar to finish his adobo and went to check the front door.

"Hi, Elena." Indeed, it was Mrs. Fairleigh.

"Rachel," Mrs. Bautista greeted nervously.

"I decided to leave early. Stephen is still held up in the city, though, so I took the bus," Mrs. Fairleigh explained. "I don't know how you tolerate the commute. Too many people and long bus lines. And it all smells terrible!" She caught the smell of Mrs. Bautista's cooking, sniffing the air then rubbing her nose into the sleeve of her flower-patterned, linen shirt. "It seems the smell followed me home. Anyways—Gareth, I'm home! Where are you, Gar?"

"I'm eating adobo," he called out from the kitchen.

"Adobo? I told you not to cook for him." Mrs. Fairleigh flared her nostrils, which finally registered the fragrance of vinegar and soy. She now realized Mrs. Bautista's defiance. "You can leave for the day, Elena."

But before Mrs. Bautista could explain, a resounding clang echoed through the house and jolted both women to run to the kitchen.

Gar was covered in vomit, a black porridge pouring out from his mouth and onto the hardwood floor. Even at a distance, Mrs. Bautista could smell the acrid vinegar-soy, stinging the back of her throat. Had she made a mistake with her recipe? Were her ratios and measurements off? She had tasted it during her cooking and tasted it when she finished. It was just as she made it for her son. She had seen the delight in Gar's face, his curious chew at first then subsequent spoonfuls of delight, no indication of anything amiss. But now, in that black pool of adobo and bits of rice speckled over it, she saw the fruits of her labor rot into the floor—she knew that the soy would stain, and the vinegar would linger in the air. She knew this couldn't be undone, that this was her own undoing.

"What did you feed him?" Mrs. Fairleigh yelled, tending to Gar with a kitchen rag.

"I'll get some soap and towels." Mrs. Bautista started for the supply closet.

"No," Mrs. Fairleigh said. "Get out, Elena. Go!"

"Yes, Ma'am—" she stammered, "I mean, Rachel. I'm sorry." She saw what used to be Gar's bowl now in broken ceramic shards in a corner of the dining room. Gar had eaten all of his serving, only to throw it back up in abjection. She remembered there was more adobo in the pot, so she walked to the stove, took the pot to the trash bin, and poured out its contents, a chef's walk of shame. This was Mark's favorite dish, Mrs. Bautista lamented, but she knew Mrs. Fairleigh would have thrown it out anyway. It was only proper that she was the one to do it, to rid their home of the evidence of her own mistake. She placed the empty pot into the sink. "I'm sorry," she repeated.

"Mom, she didn't—" Gar tried to explain.

But Mrs. Fairleigh demanded, "Leave us, now!"

After one last glance, she did, though Mrs. Bautista could hear Gareth's pleas. "She didn't do anything, she didn't do anything. Let her stay."

She had forgotten to teach Gar the other meaning of one of her adobo's ingredients. In Tagalog, suka has two meanings: the first is vinegar, and the second—vomit.

★

On the bus ride home, Mrs. Bautista thought of how to admit the day's events to her husband, how she had failed to succeed in what she set out to do. But that worry soon left her in place of another. Her thoughts returned to the scene of her crime, of the mother embracing her son in the mess she had made. Mrs. Fairleigh clung to Gareth, wiping his face and body with a linen rag; the shock on her face had simmered after her son assured her that he's fine. This image lingered in her mind, a pietà come to life.

She returned to the absence of her own home. When her husband arrived, Mrs. Bautista didn't tell him what happened. "What's wrong?" Mr. Bautista asked. What could she say to cover up her shame? Couldn't he smell the stench of Gar's vomit still on her? "What's wrong?" her husband repeated. She was wrong. Wrong to have taken the job at the Fairleighs'. Wrong to have disobeyed Rachel. Wrong to think she could replace her son with theirs. So she didn't answer.

Instead, Mrs. Bautista took up the phone, and called her son.

KAPÉ

I was reminded of my father at the coffee shop the other day. Three old Filipino men gathered around a table next to mine, taking turns to talk and sip from paper cups. I imagined it would have been liquor had they been in the homeland, like how my uncles offered me a plastic cup of rum when I was twelve years old. "Don't tell Mama," my father said, allowing me the single shot before shooing me back into the tin-can shanty. My father sat outside with his brothers, not minding the mosquitoes swirling around their heads. They were roasting a pig on a spit, embers blistering its skin, a greasy caramel brown. They drank like men at war, exchanging stories of childhood and then of their adult lives. My father had missed much in between, when he moved with his wife and child to a country not their own. He had missed his brothers.

At the cafe, the three old men looked like them, sipping cups of coffee that emboldened them, a picturesque tableau of a memory halfway around the world. "Pare!" The three men jostled each other around the coffee table, laughing,

"I swear it happened!" One of their longwinded stories had finally reached its punchline. One of them even resembled my father—a rotund man with beefy arms shaped by decades of farm work and a stomach swollen by beer. His porous, sunbaked face was as hardened as the land he had toiled. His caffeine-shot leg stirred the air beneath the table.

When we left the Philippines for suburban New Jersey, my farmer-father came with us. If he couldn't work the land with his own hands, he put his labor into the house. A small backyard garden, the laundry, the cooking, the dishes. When the toilet wouldn't flush, he argued with my mother about calling a plumber: "Ako na! I'll do it myself!" When the old coffeemaker had brewed its last cup, he showed me how to make poor man's coffee out of rice. "A farmer works for every grain," he reminded me. "Not one grain wasted." In a skillet, he toasted spoonfuls of rice, then steeped the darkened grains in warm water. A few minutes later, he drained the liquid into a cup. He let me take the first sip—my eyes widened, mesmerized by the curious concoction. But my childish excitement quickly turned sour. "This tastes like dirt!" I spewed. My father drank the rest. It was enough to last him for the day.

And yet I've since grown to love coffee, the only acceptable adult drug consumed in broad daylight, in plain sight. Black and bitter, closer to the earth. It keeps me awake and away from the dreams that make others lost boys—perhaps my father was one of them; America had been his Neverland. But when I found myself in a coffee shop in the company of three old Filipino men, I was reminded of my father and where he came from. I thought of the farmer harvesting coffee in the homeland, the beans exported elsewhere and enjoyed by someone else. Light, medium, or dark roast, like my father's changing complexion alongside the seasons, because a farmer's tan doesn't last forever. Then I was reminded of myself, the farmer's son, who never learned how to ride the carabao. As those old men finished their drinks and left with arms around each other's shoulders, I thought of how memory, like coffee, stains us all.

A STATE OF GRACE

EMERGENCY, the news stream announced on his cellphone. Jaime didn't have a television in his new apartment, and he didn't plan on paying for service. It was a rather empty studio apartment downtown, a cheap mattress on a metal frame, a foldable plastic table with four matching chairs meant for outdoor picnics. It was on the third floor in a complex with no elevator, and having made the move alone, Jaime had no care for furniture. He was happy with what he had, which wasn't much.

"What will your guests say about you?" his mother said, calling immediately when he texted her pictures of the apartment.

"What guests?" he replied. "It's just me." At least, if the hurricane was for the worse, he'd have nothing to lose.

The news stream switched between the Louisiana governor and the mayor-president of Lafayette parish. He still wasn't used to that: where he had come from—New Jersey—Jaime called them "counties," not "parishes." Parishes were for churches, and Jaime hadn't been to church since high school.

"Is there a church nearby?" his mother had asked when he moved. "You should know where the nearest church is, and the nearest hospital and grocery store. But church most of all. Maybe you'll find a nice girl there."

By girl, she meant a specific type of girl— Filipino. Jaime knew his mother's ploys, like when she hosted a rosary group in their apartment soon after he stopped going to Sunday mass. All old nanays: Filipino women whose rosaries were blessed by the Pope and whose perfume smelled of rose petals that lingered when they left. One day, a nanay brought along a granddaughter, whom Jaime thought was cute enough but who later confessed that she had no interest in him, that she was just participating in an elaborate plan between their mothers to lure him back to God. "She could have been the one," Jaime's mother would say from time to time.

But Jaime was no prodigal son, which was why, when he had the chance to, he moved as far as possible from his mother and her evangelizing. Unlike for college, where he was a commuter rather than a resident—"Take the bus," his mother had said, "you'll save much more money"—he chose a grad school in a different state, in a different latitude much closer to the equator, where hurricanes were more frequent than snow.

When he first arrived in Lafayette, he thought there were more Filipinos around. The flag of Acadiana had an uncanny resemblance to the flag of the Philippines. Both sported the same colors and similar geometric design: a white triangle jutting into the upper blue banner and the bottom red. But the Acadian flag differed in detail—a single gold star rather than an eight-rayed sun, and embellishments of three silver fleurs-de-lis and a gold Castilian tower. On his way to class at the university, he passed the flag every day; Lafayette was covered in it. He knew that flag wasn't the flag of his country, despite the resemblance. He'd get used to it like everything else about the city, he told himself. Eventually.

Jaime decided to defy the governor's orders. He opened the door into the hurricane. Where would he go? A question always on his mind. He could go down the stairs and walk the empty streets, an easy stroll through downtown and back. But there would be flooding, and he didn't know how to swim. Instead, like all things whipped up into the storm, Jaime went up.

Jaime stood on the roof, and sat some, all through the night, a nomad waiting to move. But he remained in his spot, though the maelstrom tried its best. He spoke none but hummed a tune to himself and God, whom he assumed, if there was one, was there in the middle of it all. The gusts that swung against him, the dust-confetti in

97

their swing. The flash of white against the dark horizon, the clamor in translation from sight to sound. The city was below, its stoplights swinging from their posts, red and green flickering in concert. Lafayette, whose flag resembled a country of islands halfway across the world. Islands battered by Pacific winds rather than Atlantic, called typhoons rather than hurricanes. When he was a boy in the Philippines, his parents took him to a church, Our Lady of Guidance, to whom his countrymen and women prayed in times of storm. Why not pray, then, on the roof of his new apartment? Try this time, he told himself, praying to God that he made the right choice moving to Lafayette. He worked a poem into his prayer: *Rage, rage against the dying of the light...* Was this what it meant to be a Ragin' Cajun? He found himself in that dying light, the literal blackout of stoplights and lamp posts below. It must have been God or something of the absolute. In other words, a state of—

★

"Grace," she introduced herself to Jaime. She and her mother were moving into the second floor below his; a tree had fallen onto their house during the storm and it was going through repairs, which would take at least a few months. Grace was going door to door, handing out zip-locked cookies she baked herself to her new neighbors. Her hair was cut short, her bangs held back with a folded blue bandana, and she wore a plain white T-shirt with overalls. She also had brown skin and a similar set of eyes to his, and before Jaime could ask, Grace asked him. "Filipino?"

"Very much so," he answered.

"Me too." She smiled. When Jaime met other Filipinos, he usually nodded as a recognition of their shared roots. But as Jaime and Grace acknowledged that they were indeed kababayan, there was no nod nor any other movement. They locked eyes and stared in a silence that went for too long. "O-K," she said, breaking. "I'll see you around."

"Alright, thanks." He closed the door, knowing that he liked her in an instant. She mentioned being a schoolteacher at a Catholic school, and he—a grad student teaching college freshmen—entertained the coupling of educators. Jaime had a habit of reading into potential matches; if anyone would have a say in "The One," it would be him and not his mother.

Soon after their meeting, he came home from classes and found Grace unloading boxes from her car. Jaime sprung at his chance. "Need any help?" he asked.

"Oh yes," she said, peeking out from behind the large cargo box in her hands. "Thanks, Jaime." His stomach stirred at her remembering his name. He took the cargo box from her, which was a familiar kind of box; his parents had the same kind to send goods back to the Philippines—balikbayan boxes, they were called, that which returns to the country.

Grace picked up a smaller box and led Jaime up the stairs. "These are only temporary things, essentials, until we get back to the house." Despite her words, Jaime, his arms flexing at ninety degrees against the cargo, imagined he and Grace were moving in together. He lent himself to the fantasy until a misstep up the stairs broke it.

"You okay?" she asked.

"Yup," he said, catching himself on the last step before the second floor. He tried to suppress his exasperated breathing, which made him suffer all the more.

"Don't expect much." Grace turned the key into the door. "We—well, my mom is still deciding where to put things."

"You should see my apartment." Shit, he thought to himself, too much, too desperate. "I didn't mean it like—"

As she pushed the door open, Jaime heard the familiar voice of a Filipino nanay, an accent of superiority strung together with motherly love.

"Sino yan?" Grace's mother entered the living room, surprised to see a young man inside. "Hay! May lalake."

"Nay." Grace inflected her voice like a child, a plea to stop the embarrassment. "This is Jaime. He lives upstairs."

"Hi," Jaime said, the box still in his grip. The nanay's eyes were fixed on him, dark brown targets that pinned him on the spot. Eager to break her stare before the cargo box broke him, he spoke up, quivering, "Where should I put this?"

"Right here is fine," Grace said. He set the box down next to hers. She was already unpacking her box, unwrapping a small object from a bundle of newspapers. When it was fully unwrapped, Jaime knew it immediately—a miniature statue of Jesus as a brown child, a Santo Niño. A similar one sat on an altar back at his parents' house. She handed it to her mother, who took the statue into the kitchen, a separate room with a pass-through window into the living room so Jaime could still feel her stare.

"So, Jaime." Grace's mother pronounced his name the way his own mother called him, the J as an H, Hi-meh rather than Jay-me—he'd gone by the American pronunciation since his family immigrated, but his mother kept to the original, much like other things she brought from the motherland. He saw his mother in Grace's, a woman who had grown old but never weak, modeled herself after the Virgin Mary, wiping down the Santo Niño with a damp paper towel as if the Christ child were hers. "What are you doing in Lafayette?"

"I go to the university," he answered. "For my master's."

"Engineering? Chemistry?"

"No, uh…" He was always insecure in admitting this part, especially to other Filipinos, and especially to the Filipino mother of the girl he was crushing on. "English."

"Oh," she said with the same disappointment he heard from his mother when he revealed his college major and, later, graduate course of study. To her, the humanities were inextricably tied to lower salaries. "The same with Grace. She studied history."

"If by the same you mean not nursing," Grace interjected. "Nay's disappointed I didn't become a nurse like her."

"At least you became a teacher," her mother said. "Good enough for you."

Grace held in a breath, rolled her eyes; *You mean good enough for YOU*, Jaime understood.

She was unboxing the larger box, uncovering notebooks, planners, textbooks, even a printer—this was life in the humanities, Jaime knew, carrying around a variety of Norton anthologies on his back, Sisyphus in every step. He was happy to bear that burden for Grace for a short while. It was juvenile, the way a teenage boy carried a girl's backpack, but romance was always juvenile.

"Is there anything else I can do?" Jaime asked. Between Grace and her mother, he was a balloon in a stack of needles.

"I think we can manage—"

"Yes, Jaime," her mother accepted eagerly. "We only had the movers for a day, and they had no care for interior design. You can help me move these where they belong." She gestured for him to push the furniture to the side of the living room.

"You really don't have to," Grace assured him. But Jaime couldn't help but try to impress her and, a bonus, her mother, thinking ahead to when he would need her blessing as her daughter's suitor.

Their apartment wasn't a studio like his. It had two bedrooms, the smaller one for Grace and the larger one for her mother. There were separate bed frames and mattresses for each of them, three dressers, two bookshelves, a couch, a dining table and smaller ones. Jaime tried his best to follow their instructions, moving one piece of furniture from one wall to the other, one corner to its opposite, between Grace's "over there" and her mother's "no, no—doon, diyan, yes!" He had cheated himself of this experience with his own apartment, moving in with plastic chairs and plastic bins, a discounted mattress on a metal frame. When both women reached an agreement and one piece of furniture was set firmly in place,

Jaime snuck a successful smile toward Grace, who received it with an amusing slow clap.

He knew they were finished when Grace's mother set the Santo Niño on a table, consecrating it an altar in one corner of the living room.

"Perfect," her mother said. "Okay na for Sunday."

"We're getting the apartment blessed," Grace explained. "Even though this place is temporary."

"All homes are temporary," her mother said, "which is why you have to take care of every place you live in and get it blessed." Jaime nodded, not wanting to confess the poor condition of his own apartment. "You should come, Jaime, yes?"

He looked over to Grace. She shrugged.

"There will be a big party and lots of food," her mother stressed. "Pancit, lumpia, and lechon! Sige na—consider it our thank you for all your help."

He didn't want to attend any religious gathering, but he really liked Grace. The food, too, would be a welcome reward for his moving services. He hadn't had good, greasy Filipino food since he left for Lafayette, only instant ramen and microwavable meal trays.

"Yes," Jaime said. "Sige."

He didn't expect the elder woman's embrace, thin but fortified arms hugging him, her graying hair brushing against his chin as she leaned into his chest. She was about the same height as his mother. When he was released from her hold, he half-hoped Grace would follow up with her own embrace, sadly to no avail.

"Let me walk you to your apartment," she said instead.

"Goodbye, Jaime," her mother said, again with a silent J in her native tongue. "See you Sunday!"

They made their way up to the floor above, Jaime leading Grace to his door this time.

"You don't have to go to the blessing if you don't want to," Grace said. "My mom likes to pressure every boy I meet into these things."

"I understand," Jaime said. "My mother's the same—controlling."

"Yes, that's the word," she said. "Controlling."

They returned to the awkward silence from their initial meeting, the moment of goodbye when neither wanted to say it.

"I'll go to the blessing," Jaime said, breaking the silence. "If that's okay with you?"

The edge of her mouth piqued a half-smile. "I'll see you Sunday."

★

There was a mass before the blessing, but Jaime didn't go. It was Sunday after all, and he usually slept in, which he did that morning. He rolled out of bed at 11:30 a.m., enough time, he thought, to get ready for the noon gathering downstairs.

He showered and brushed, styled his hair back with pomade, and put on a button-down shirt and khakis—loose, professional clothing he wore when he taught and attended his classes. Jaime eyed his outfit in the mirror, knowing full well his mother would have sent him directly to the tailor to get his clothes fitted. He loved wearing clothes that would upset her now that she was no longer there to chide him. He even considered a tattoo. Whatever he wore on a Sunday would be his Sunday best. He finished getting ready at noon exactly, and left his apartment for Grace's without making his bed—he loved that part of his new life too.

He didn't expect the gathering to have started, the 10 a.m. mass only ending an hour earlier. But it seemed that the entire congregation—all Filipinos—followed Grace and her mother home immediately. He could already hear the music and conversations, and on his way down, the neighbors too began to notice.

"What's going on there?" one neighbor asked Jaime as he passed by.

"A house blessing," Jaime said.

"Oh, really?" The neighbor seemed more enthused than disgruntled. "They're getting their apartment blessed, hun," he yelled inside his own apartment. "Why didn't we ever get ours blessed?" And with that, the neighbor retreated indoors, his curiosity satisfied. The other neighbors followed suit.

The door to the apartment was open, people trailing in. As he entered, the others acknowledged Jaime with their eyes, to which he nodded, everyone already familiar with a sense of Filipino-ness otherwise absent from his daily life in the city. He also smelled that familiar rose scented perfume, and sure enough, he spotted all the Filipino nanays seated in the midst of tsismis. Yesterday, he wouldn't have thought of fitting more than fifty people into their apartment, but there they were, parents and children, the Filipino congregation of Lafayette and the surrounding areas. Regardless of his falling out with the faith, Jaime fit right in.

He could already smell the food, and all along the kitchen counter and dining table, Jaime saw the banquet. Two large rice cookers, hefty trays of pancit and lumpia, and—the centerpiece—lechon, a whole roasted pig, its crispy skin glistening like glass, waiting to be broken into. There were also the desserts laid out on a separate table: leche flan, cassava cake, ube cake. Was he in the Deep South, or transported back to his childhood home where they celebrated birthdays and Christmases with the same sweet and savory menu?

"There you are." Grace tapped him on the shoulder. "We're about to start." Her Sunday best was also more laidback than his mother, and her mother too, would have approved—a plaid button-down rather than a white T-shirt, tucked into the same overalls. Rather than a bandana, her bangs were clipped to the side with a hairpin. Even then, Jaime was infatuated.

She took his hand and pulled him through the crowd—the number of people inside again surprising him. They found themselves in a clearing at the center of the living room, where the altar with the Santo Niño was placed. The Christ child had new ornaments: colored flower petals wrapped around his neck. Beside the altar stood Grace's mother—wearing a white Maria Clara dress, its high shoulder pads almost eclipsing her head—and a Filipino priest, young, clean-shaven, and bald, dressed down in black and a white collar. Grace's mother gestured for Grace and Jaime to join them in front of the altar.

"Jaime." Her mother took his hands from Grace, kissing him on each cheek. "Father, this is Jaime. He's the one who helped us move in."

"Jaime," the priest called him, also with the authentic pronunciation. "Blessed are you. I'm Father Dominic. The parishioners call me Father Dom."

"Nice to meet you, Father Dom," Jaime said uncomfortably—he never liked calling other men by Father; family they were not.

"And you already know my daughter, Grace." Her mother pushed Grace forward to greet Father Dom.

"Yes, hello, Grace." The priest shook her hand, which Grace pulled back as soon as he finished.

"Okay, good! Nandito na ang lahat," her mother exclaimed. "We're ready to begin, Father." She clapped her hands and waved to the others from one side of the room to the next, letting everyone know it was time for the ceremony. The conversations soon simmered, hushed voices turned silent, a nanay threatened a whining child with an extended, flattened hand, which would do instead of the typical flip flop. Jaime, standing next to Grace, met her eyes, both suppressing laughter at the scene they had experienced as children of Filipino mothers.

"Brothers and sisters," Father Dom began. "Today we are gathered at the blessing of Ginang Mara and her daughter's new home. Let us pray..." He proceeded to recite a blessing from a three-ring binder, probably a ready-made blessing he recited at every house warming, Jaime thought. The priest retrieved a bottle of holy water and raised it, splashing it on the altar, then around the room. While they followed Father Dom into each room, Jaime let the priest's words turn to white noise, thinking, as he stood next to Grace, that the ceremony could have been their pseudo wedding. He relished the moment until his ears perked up at Father Dom's final words, "On behalf of Ginang Mara, her daughter Grace, and Grace's *boyfriend*, thank you for coming." Grace retracted her hand to hide her face, blushing red. Jaime, too, felt his cheeks go warm. He wasn't her boyfriend, or at least, not yet. Their embarrassment only lasted a moment—thank God—as Grace's mother announced, "Kain na tayo!" rallying the congregation to the food.

★

"How long have you been in Lafayette?" Father Dom asked him at the table. Jaime sat next to Grace, who sat next to her mother, who sat next to the priest. He would have been content to keep quiet while his mouth was occupied with food—he would have indulged in it—if not for Father Dom's interrogation, pulling out a confession.

"A few months," he said. "I got here in the summer, then began school right away."

"Ah, I see," the priest responded. "So, recently. No wonder I haven't seen you at church."

"Well, I also don't have a car to get there," Jaime added in defense. "I walk to class and back."

"Puwes—I can arrange for the church bus to pick you up."

"Uh-hm." Jaime swallowed his bite, the fat from the roasted pig still a chunk, which he forced down uncomfortably.

"Yes, good idea, Father!" Grace's mother added.

He looked at Grace, who had been silent until then but was now giggling to herself. She raised her eyes at Jaime and nodded. While he slid into his seat, Grace was having fun.

"Actually, Father," her mother continued, "Jaime's apartment is just above us. Maybe you can do another blessing?"

Panic ran through Jaime's body, the grease from all the rice and pork unsettling his stomach. Grace kicked his foot gently, laughing to herself behind her plate. She was enjoying this.

"Of course!" The priest put his plate down and stood up. "Jaime, would you lead us to your apartment?"

Grace stared at Jaime, waiting for his next move, amused.

"Yeah, uhm." Put on the spot, having already eaten the food, pierced by the eager eyes of Grace's mother, Jaime had no choice. "Okay, I'll take us up."

By "us," Jaime only meant Father Dom, Grace, and her mother. He didn't expect the others to stop their conversations, put their plates down, and follow them up to his apartment, per Grace's mother's instructions. "Tara na," she announced, raising her hand like a tour guide as she followed Jaime out the door.

"I hope you know what you got yourself into," Grace said, following beside him, nudging his shoulder with hers.

Under his breath, clear enough for Grace to hear but not for the others, he lamented, "Fuck me."

"Eto na?" Grace's mother asked as Jaime stopped in front of his door.

"This is it." He turned the key and let them in.

"Oh," she said. Grace's mother reacted the way he imagined his mother would—with shock and disappointment. Of course, had it been his mother, she would have lashed out, pushing Jaime to attend to his cheap bed, pointing out the ruffled sheets, telling him to take the dirty laundry off of it and to sort it out in a laundry basket; she would have smelled the musty, heavy air and opened a window, kicked the empty frozen food boxes to the side, and told him to pick up the trash and take it out; his mother would have left moments after, gone to a store, and brought back a trove of cleaning supplies. Instead, Grace's mother held in her impulses, dragging out her frustrations in another "Ooohhh."

"Looks like the hurricane came through your apartment, Jaime," Father Dom said. "It's going to need a little extra prayer today."

Jaime unfolded the plastic picnic chairs for the nanays, urging them to take a seat despite the clear disgust on their faces. One of them produced a perfume bottle and spritzed the air. Jaime held in his cough, suffocated in roses. Because his apartment was a studio, the whole congregation didn't fit. But many didn't bother coming inside after seeing its condition; they remained on the balcony outside, hoping for the blessing to end quickly.

And it did end quickly. There weren't other rooms besides the bed/living/dining room, so Father Dom merely stood in the center, reciting the same prayer from his binder, splashing holy water at each of the four walls. Grace's mother stood next to the seated nanays, while Grace held Jaime's hand, still hiding her laughter under her breath. He wondered if she was also laughing at his apartment in its state of disrepair, if she thought it was a lackluster reflection of him.

"Amen," the priest concluded, much to everyone's relief. The nanays were first to leave, Grace's mother among them. Before leaving with the rest, Father Dom told Jaime, "Prayer goes a long way, but so does making your bed, cleaning up your home. Cleanliness on the outside, cleanliness on the inside." He pointed to Jaime's heart. On his way out, he continued, "I hope to see you at church, Jaime." Jaime merely nodded.

Grace stayed with Jaime. They were finally alone.

"Your mother's disappointed in me," he said.

"I know the feeling," she said. "I like what you've done with the place," she added sarcastically.

"It's just me here," he said, repeating what he had told his mother. "First time living on my own, no one telling me what to do. Simple living. And I wasn't expecting guests."

"I love Nay and all," she said, "but she follows wherever I go. Sometimes I wish for that simple living."

Not wanting to subject her to any more of his apartment's rugged torment, Jaime thought of taking Grace elsewhere. "Have you been on the roof?"

★

It had been a week since the hurricane, since Jaime found himself alone on that roof, raging against the whirlwind of night. Now he sat next to Grace, their legs dangling off the edge. Had it been a weekday, the city below would have been alive with suits and skirts, lawyers, bankers, locals frequenting their café of choice. It was almost like New York—a sample size. Jaime used to think he'd settle in the Big Apple after college. But Lafayette had its own hue of sun, its own leisurely pace. New York would have still been buzzing, even on a Sunday. There were plenty of bike riders like the larger city, but Lafayette had more trucks and fewer yellow cabs. The air was clearer in breath and sight, the sky less scraped by glass and steel. He described these differences to Grace, telling her his life story, where he came from and how he got here.

"I was born in the Philippines," he added like a footnote. "I was only four when we left for Jersey. There's not much I can tell you about it since then."

Then Jaime remembered how some of the first Filipinos in America came to Louisiana. When he was younger, Jaime often viewed himself as the first of his kind, having immigrated as a boy, grown up American but not really, raised Filipino but not really. He kept up his schoolwork for his parents, knowing their measure of his success was a measure of their leap of American faith. He had never thought of himself as one of a long lineage of Filipino Americans, that is until a visiting professor came to his college during Filipino American History Month in October and told him about the fishermen who jumped ship to escape the Spanish and settled in the bayous. "You wouldn't happen to know Dr. Arturo Rosales?" he asked Grace, remembering the professor's name.

"Of course I know Arturo Rosales—I read his book!" Grace echoed much of Professor Arturo's lecture about the Manila Men of Louisiana, but Jaime loved seeing her excitement and passion, too. "You don't really learn about them in textbooks, which is why I always begin the school year with that fact. I introduce myself to the high schoolers, 'Ms. Cruz,'"—she put on her teacherly persona—"then I throw them that fun fact as if it's a fact about myself." She introduced more of her story to Jaime, how her mother immigrated as a nurse, married an accountant who left her when Grace was born. "It was always just me and Nay. She took care of me, and now I take care of her, though she wouldn't say that exactly. To her, she's still taking care of me."

"Even after moving here," Jaime said, "I can still hear my mother telling me to make my bed, to throw out the trash. I don't, of course, as you already saw."

"Mhmm." Grace nudged his shoulder. Jaime feigned falling off the edge, only kidding.

He continued, "Sometimes I feel like there are hidden cameras in my apartment. Because she's still there, Mama. As long as there's a mess, she's still there."

"Do you like Louisiana?" she asked.

"So far," he answered. "It's definitely different from what I'm used to. Don't get me started with all the French words and last names. I butcher all of them."

"That's Acadiana for you," Grace explained. "Some people pass through, others stay, like the French Canadians years ago, or like me and Nay. That's just life: a hurricane. You'll never know where you'll land. At least that's how I think of it."

"You're starting to sound like me," he said, finding confidence in his comfort with her. "Metaphor and life. My love language." *Yuck.* "Sorry," he said immediately, embarrassed by his attempt at flirting.

"Don't be." Grace kissed him on the cheek, and he was reminded of the hurricane, its raw power to convince him of some higher force at work in the universe. He felt the fulfillment of belonging where one has never belonged, where the outsider finds the inherent. It was juvenile; it was romantic. "I better get back. Nay's probably wondering where I went."

He walked her to her apartment, where the crowd had shrunk. Father Dom had already left, and her mother was talking to the few remaining nanays. Jaime helped Grace clean up the plastic plates and cups, then packed up the leftover foods in Ziploc bags and Tupperware. As the remaining guests left, Grace's mother offered them the leftovers, and as Jaime started for the door, he received the rest. "Your reward, Jaime." She handed them to him with some parting words, "After you clean your room, ha?" Jaime nodded. She was laughing, but he knew she meant every word.

"Wait," Grace said. She went to her room and came back with a book in hand. She patted away the dust and handed it to Jaime. He read the cover,

The Manila Men of Louisiana by Arturo Rosales. "Something to help you feel more at home."

"Thanks," he said. "I'll be sure to return it."

When Grace led him out the door and made sure they were out of her mother's sight, she hugged Jaime. "I'll see you around."

Jaime came back to his dilapidated apartment, newly blessed. He briefly considered making his bed, doing the laundry, and vacuuming. He put Dr. Rosales' book on his nightstand, then placed his packed leftovers in the fridge, a Filipino feast that would last him for the next few days, saving him from the expense of cheap frozen foods. Then the scent of roses struck him, the scent of the nanays and their Pope-blessed rosaries. "Clean your room," Jaime heard his mother's voice in his head. So, he took up the pile of clothes on his bed and folded them, started a new load for his dirty ones in the laundry, and changed his sheets. Between the stress and anxiety of attending Grace and her mother's apartment blessing and his own impromptu one, Jaime was relieved to have lasted through the day. As he lay on his freshly made bed, the scent of roses still in the air, Jaime thought of home.

"I got my apartment blessed," Jaime said when he called his mother. "And I met a girl...a Filipino girl," he confessed.

"So my prayers worked," she said, proudly. Though, from her tone, Jaime knew she meant

"I told you so." It was as if it was because of his mother he had moved to Lafayette—which was partly true—as if she herself had conjured up the hurricane, which led him to meet Grace, like it had been all part of her plan.

EVERYTHING MUST STAY

One Sunday afternoon, just as the congregation filed out of church and into the street, the word spread that Miguel's Sari-Sari Store was closing. "First his wife, now his store," Clara said.

"It's *because* of his wife the store is closing," Paulina explained—she, apparently, had the inside scoop. "He's refusing to agree to the divorce. He's been using his life savings to pay a lawyer, but by now he's run out of options." Though gossip was typical in these after-church discussions, Miguel and Juanita Gonzaga's divorce wasn't at all the typical tsismis those days.

Sure, there had been affairs and marriage problems in the past, among other neighborly private matters. For example, a year prior, there was the rumor about Mrs. Carol DeAngelo, a widow who lived in the apartment above the sari-sari store. She, allegedly, was running a pop-up brothel every other weekend, taking in young men and women in the middle of the night. Only later, after she passed, did the truth come out: her grand-nieces and -nephews had been visiting and paying their respects to the woman in anticipation of her death. "I never believed it," Paulina said about the brothel rumor, though she was convinced before.

"I always had the highest regard for Mrs. DeAngelo," Clara added, feigning condolences, "She was such a strong woman."

But rumors like the one about Carol DeAngelo never interfered with the lives of others. Gossip was only fun if it was about someone else and had nothing to do with them. The recent revelation surrounding Miguel and Juanita's divorce was shocking, not because they had been together for decades and had been successfully raising two children, but because the closing of their sari-sari store would have a direct impact on the neighborhood around it and, more specifically, on Clara and Paulina. It was the only Filipino store in the city, and the other Asian markets were miles in opposite directions. The private matter of Miguel and Juanita Gonzaga's divorce had now become a very serious, public matter.

This time, Clara and Paulina decided to verify the news for themselves. They had heard that the store was having a closeout sale on its final weekend, and the two women couldn't help but take advantage.

"We should hurry," Paulina said, "before they run out of my chicharon!" The sari-sari stocked a specific kind of chicharon—not just fried pig skin, but fried pig skin with some pork meat still attached. Despite her doctor's orders to stay away from such heart-attack-inducing snacks, Paulina took every opportunity to treat herself. Besides, the store was closing. She would give them up after she exhausted the Gonzagas' final supply.

Clara, on the other hand, didn't want anything so gratuitous as chicharon. Instead, she wanted to stock up on her Belo Beauty products. She'd been mailing some to her daughter Emily to help brighten up her skin. "I need some soap for my daughter," Clara told Paulina. "She unfortunately took after her father. And the sun is particularly strong in Florida."

Paulina agreed. "In *fair*-ness, no one has skin as beautiful as yours, my dear."

Clara couldn't help but tease her friend. "Maybe you would, too, if you stopped eating that chicharon!"

Paulina stopped in her tracks and glared at her. But she couldn't stay mad at Clara too long— her sullen frown dissolved into a smile, and then a laugh. Clara joined in her friend's amusement. It was a good joke after all. On their walk to the store, Paulina pointed out how similar they actually were: "We are women who love pig fat, just with different applications."

Like church, the fact that the sari-sari was an essential part of the neighborhood was what brought Clara and Paulina together in the first place. When Clara first moved into that part of the city, she came as a single mother with her daughter Emily. Her husband, it turned out, was raising a secret second family back in the Philippines, where he sent remittances. When Clara told her mother-in-law about the money, she said she'd never received any payments from her son. When Clara confronted him, her husband folded. She left him immediately, filing for divorce and taking Emily with her. Miguel's Sari-Sari Store was the first place she took her daughter after moving. Emily was five then, and she packed as many chichirya she could fit between her chubby, albeit stout, arms.

"That's a lot of chips. The chicharon is my favorite!" Paulina had said. She approached Clara and Emily. "You're new here, right?"

"Yes—I just left my husband," Clara said simply.

"Oh," Paulina replied, "*Ooohhh*—then we should celebrate!" After some brief introductions, Paulina took Clara and her daughter under her wing, even paying for all of Emily's chips. She invited them over to her apartment, where they spent the night singing songs from a karaoke machine, ignoring the neighbors who came knocking at her door to complain. Since then, Clara looked to Paulina as her best friend. Paulina, too, had no husband—an ex-nun-in-training, a runaway novitiate. In their twenty years of friendship, and with Emily now in Florida, Clara and Paulina only had each other.

As they approached the site of their first meeting, they found that they weren't the only ones anticipating the closeout sale at the sari-sari. A crowd had formed around the entire block and spilled onto the street. As they approached closer, they could see why. There were cops stationed outside the storefront, their cars and barricades holding off the eager shoppers determined to buy out the Gonzagas' remaining stock of miscellaneous dry goods and beauty products. Clara and Paulina pushed themselves through the crowd and stood their ground behind the barricade. "We're not looters," Clara said under her breath.

"Hey, what's all this?" Paulina asked one of the officers keeping the crowd at bay. She always had a way with people.

"Hostage situation."

"*Hostage situation?*" the two women echoed in disbelief.

"A teenage girl is keeping herself and brother locked up in there."

"Susmaryosep."

The girl and boy must have been the Gonzaga children, Alexandra and Matty. When Alexandra was younger, Clara's daughter used to babysit her. Emily always spoke highly of her: not one ounce of stubbornness, always on top of her homework. When Alexandra got older and began working the register at the sari-sari, she always welcomed Clara with respect and familiarity. "You remember me, right?" Clara reminded her every time, "My daughter used to babysit you when you were this small! You tell your parents I said hi, okay? Tell them Tita Clara said hi." Alexandra smiled and said that she would, though Clara never followed up—neither she nor Paulina were that close with the Gonzagas. The last time they saw them all together at church was for their son's baptism. Matty was now five. The family's absence at church since was a telltale sign of the Gonzagas' crumbling marriage and faith.

Some distance away from the store was its owner, Miguel Gonzaga, speaking with a group of police officers. Whatever hair he had left was greasy and scattered around his crown, and there were bags like inkblots under his eyes. He looked like he hadn't taken a shower in weeks, frazzled and depressed. Who wouldn't look that way with his wife having left him, his store closing down, and his own children keeping each other as hostages?

A local news van pulled up next to the crowd. A reporter and cameraman jumped right out and began filming, setting up a perfectly framed shot in front of the sign that read Miguel's Sari-Sari Store and the big Everything Must Go poster that hung on the window.

"Visitors arrived at this store today expecting their favorite Filipino items on sale," the reporter began, "but the children of this mom-and-pop store had other plans. More on this developing story in just a few minutes." This must have been the most attention the neighborhood had ever received from the rest of the city. The fact that the reporter came from a national station was all the more exciting. The spotlight was on them.

"How do I look?" Paulina asked.

"Could be worse."

"*Gago*—what the hell do you mean by that?"

"I'm joking, I'm joking," Clara said. "You look...exquisite. Dr. Vicki Belo would be proud."

"This isn't a joking matter, Clara. This is a *hostage situation* and we're on live TV!"

Paulina gestured toward the cameraman, who was now panning across the crowd. Both women did their best to find their good side, leaning left then right then left again. They must have done a great job at voguing because they caught the reporter's attention and he approached them. The cameraman followed them to the barricade.

"Would you like to provide some words on camera?" he asked the women.

"*Yes,*" they said emphatically.

They would go live in one minute, the reporter informed them. But that minute might as well have been fifteen. Clara retrieved a makeup bag from her purse and produced a compact to apply powder on her face, as if she could get any fairer than her Belo Beauty skin would allow. Without asking, Paulina took a lipstick from Clara's makeup bag, though her friend was unbothered. They shared the same compact mirror to look at themselves. When Paulina's lipstick was out of line, Clara wiped the burgundy smudge away. Then, when Clara was finished with the powder, she exchanged the brush with the lipstick. Paulina, too, added powder to her face.

"How do I look *now*?" Paulina asked.

"Like a clown," Clara said with a smirk.

Before Paulina could respond, the reporter was counting down from five.

"I am in front of Miguel's Sari-Sari Store where the owner's children have locked themselves inside in rebellion. Their cause? Their parents' divorce. Alexandra, seventeen, and Matty, only five, are refusing to open the doors unless their mother Juanita Gonzaga reunites with their father. I am joined by some of the community members here who might have some inside information on the situation." He turned his attention to Paulina first. "Miss, what do you know of the Gonzagas and how did all this escalate?"

"Well, sir, I think all of this began when the wife left her husband for the Philippines," Paulina began. She tried her best American accent, channeling a pageant queen. "I heard it was a very unhappy marriage."

"Are you saying the owner of the store, Miguel Gonzaga, is some kind of—"

"Susmaryosep!" Paulina took a moment to compose herself. She didn't expect the reporter to take his job so seriously. "I am not insinuating such a thing. In fairness, I admire Miguel Gonzaga and what he has done for us. He is a pillar of this community." Though she didn't totally mean those words, Paulina was proud of her performance. She could already envision herself on TV—such a poised, articulate woman standing up for a beloved neighbor. She was incredibly proud of her use of "insinuating" and "pillar." Besides, if Miguel had heard her comments, he might give her a discount on, or perhaps even free, chicharron for defending his name and reputation.

"What about you, miss?" It was Clara's turn. "Why do you think the children have taken such extreme measures?"

"I know Alexandra," Clara began. "My daughter Emily was her babysitter some years ago. I never heard a bad thing about her. She reminds me of Emily in many ways. Miguel and Juanita are lucky to have her and Matty as children." Her intent was less performative and rather genuine. She took a moment to add to her response, "As a parent, I know how strong the bond between mother and child can be. I believe Alexandra just wants her mother back. Juanita Gonzaga—if you are listening—your children need you."

Just as Clara finished her response, as if on cue, Alexandra Gonzaga and her brother Matty appeared behind the storefront window. The cameraman turned toward the scene, where the children's father was now pounding on the glass, asking them to open the door. But they ignored him. Instead, Alexandra took down the Everything Must Go poster and placed it on the floor. She and her brother bent down over it. "The children seem to be writing down a message," the reporter narrated. When the children stood back up and the poster re-emerged, their message was apparent. "The sign now reads Everything Must *STAY*. Their intentions are clear. They do not want their family's store to close. But could this be yet another message to their mother? Will she make an appearance and give into her children's demands? We'll keep you updated." The reporter signed off.

"My feet are beginning to hurt," Paulina said, completely unbothered by the new revelation. Besides, the camera was no longer on them. So they decided to leave for Paulina's apartment. If all went right for the Gonzagas, and if their call-to-action was of any help, they could return to the sari-sari store tomorrow.

★

Only when they arrived at the apartment did the two women find out if the children were successful in their gamble to save their parents' marriage. Though they arrived emptyhanded, Paulina still had a bag of chicharon in her pantry. She and Clara sat on the couch, took turns digging their fingers into the salt-dusted pork rinds, and turned the television to the news. They were replaying the days' events and, just as they expected, Paulina's and Clara's faces filled up the screen. With their matching caked-up facades, they looked just like sisters.

"The camera loves us," Paulina said, pointing at the screen.

"We really are beautiful," Clara admitted.

When Paulina suggested that she let her daughter know about it, Clara texted Emily to watch the news. She smiled at her daughter's reply. "Emily says my Belo products are really working!" Paulina was happy letting Clara text her daughter—she never was jealous; after all, she had become a default godmother to Emily since they first met at the sari-sari. Instead, Paulina was merely content that she was able to gain an extra handful of chicharon. But just as she took three pieces into her mouth, the screen flashed BREAKING NEWS. Paulina almost choked.

The crowd that remained in front of Miguel's Sari-Sari Store had now begun chanting *Everything must stay!* Then, they began to emphasize a single word: *Stay...stay...stay!* They repeated it, as if to command the very person the Gonzaga children were pleading for. *Stay...stay...stay!* Paulina put the chicharon down on a table and gestured for Clara to get off her phone and to look back at the television. The crowd parted as a woman, escorted by police, made her way through. *Stay...stay... stay!* the crowd continued, as if the children's plea was also theirs, and it was—the fate of the store was tied to Miguel and Juanita's delicate marriage. No matter the chaos around her, the woman glided through the crowd with elegance. Her brown skin was flawless, and her cheekbones were defined. Her long hair wrapped around her face comfortably like black silk. Was this some Filipino celebrity fighting off paparazzi? No. This woman was none other than Juanita Gonzaga. No wonder Miguel refused to agree to the divorce. She was beautiful. Paulina and Clara watched in awe.

"I thought you said she fled to the Philippines?" Clara said.

"I only heard about it," Paulina replied.

"We have confirmation that the children's mother, Juanita Gonzaga, has arrived on the scene," the reported announced. "The police are now leading her to the storefront to meet with her husband. We can only hope that the negotiations with their children will come next."

The couple didn't hug or show signs of affection, seemingly confirming that their marriage was, indeed, in turbulent water. Juanita was shouting at her husband, as if she were chastising him for all the events that had led to this spectacle. What did he do to make her leave in the first place? Whatever it was, he was obviously in the wrong. Miguel hung his head low, receiving the verbal beating like a big, groveling dog. To the women sitting on the couch, this was the best kind of soap opera. The only thing missing was Juanita slapping some sense into her husband's face in slow motion. When the door to the sari-sari finally opened and Alexandra and Matty ran to their parents, the teleserye had reached its logical conclusion. Juanita welcomed her children's embrace, and even tolerated Miguel's touch. A happy ending.

"Isn't that nice?" Clara pointed out.

"If this means I get to go back tomorrow for more of *these*"—Paulina had finally finished the entire bag of chicharon—"then all's well that ends well for all of us."

After the big embrace, the reporter approached the Gonzagas for some answers.

"This was all a misunderstanding." Miguel took the mic from the reporter. "The sari-sari isn't closing. We are merely renovating and reopening at a later date. The first matter of business is adding my wife's name to the sign. Because this store has really been *our* store. We are a *family* business. Isn't that right, my dear?"

"It's about damn time," was all Juanita said to the camera. She glared at her husband, then turned her attention to her children. "Let's go home." Was that really at the root of their divorce, her name omitted from the storefront?

The final events were quite anticlimactic. As Miguel closed up shop, the police ordered the crowd to disperse. Before rejoining his wife and children, Miguel assured the crowd that the store would re-open, and stay open, the next day. He apologized for the confusion. This was good news for them, and even better news for Clara and Paulina. "There you have it folks," the reporter said, "Miguel *and* Juanita's Sari-Sari Store will remain open. The community is a bit shaken, but far from broken. If there's anything we can learn from today's events, it's that the kids are alright." The final shot lingered on Juanita and her children hand-in-hand, while Miguel sprinted to catch up to them. Then the news cut to a commercial, and the two women on the couch sat in silence.

After a minute, Clara finally asked, "Should we invite Juanita for some karaoke?"

"She'll need a lot more than karaoke if she's going to stay with her husband," Paulina said. "God bless her."

"And her children, too," Clara added.

Clara and Paulina knew that they were fortunate enough to have dodged the bullet of men throughout the years. Clara especially was lucky to have left her husband when she did; she never knew if he went back to the Philippines for his secret family, or perhaps he petitioned to have them come here—though, either way, Clara didn't care. She had done her duty as a mother to Emily, all without his help. Paulina, too, was lucky to have found a friend in Clara. This was not what either of them expected when they first left the Philippines for the States, one betrothed to a lying, deadbeat scumbag and the other an aspiring mother superior. But to Clara, Paulina became a sister, nonetheless.

So they planned to extend the invitation to Juanita the next time they swung by the sari-sari, which would now also bear her name. They would ask her out not only for a night of karaoke, but also to join them at church on Sundays. They would help Juanita live a happy life. They'd welcome her into their sisterhood—along with all the tsismis that passed through her store.

RICE KITES

Back then, we made kites out of day-old rice. We rehydrated each grain with a splash of water, and with a wooden spoon pounded the rice in a bowl until it all turned to mush. Sometimes we didn't have a spoon and only used our hands, bare knuckles splashing into last night's meal, specks of sauce from the kare kare mixed into the now yellow paste. Our younger cousins couldn't help but sneak a lick to taste—how bold of them, so easily pleased by their curiosity. They giggled at the aftertaste of faint peanut butter and bagoong. Then we took a pair of wooden barbecue skewers and lined them up into a cross like the palm leaves we were given at church around Easter time. We found pages of newspaper with yet another corrupt politician, or sheets of pastel-colored tissue paper that never made it onto last Christmas's parols. We placed the paper flat against the frame. With a piso-sized clump of the rice mixture between our fingers, we molded the paste around each intersection and corner point, hoping the skewers and paper would hold in place. We laid the contraptions out on the concrete where the sun could find them.

Eventually, the rice dried out, hardened as the grip of our parents' scolding hands after running loose in the palenke. The rice would become the glue that held our kites together. With stolen yarn from our grandmother's cookie tin, we tied knots at the end of our paper kites. By that point it had felt like a day's work, honing our craft. All that was left was the wind—that, we couldn't control. Out in the streets, we held up the kites, waiting for the promise of the summer gusts. When the warm air whistled and the mango trees swayed, it was time. We threw the crafts into the air, hoped they'd catch the wind, that the rice would hold them together in the sky. Then we watched them fly.

A BALIKBAYAN AFFAIR

The provincial saloon is nearly empty when Melinda tells her sons about their father's affair. The three of them sit in a booth near the bar, the mother facing her two sons. The boys are grown now, the elder already twenty-one and the younger nineteen. But to Melinda, they are still boys, still children—not like the broken, lonely men at the bar sitting some distance from each other. For them, the truckers and jeepney drivers en route to some other destination, there is no occasion for their drinking. But for Melinda and her boys, they are gathered for one reason, one person. It is a Sunday evening, some hours after the funeral. She has buried Mickey, her husband, six feet into Philippine soil, the same soil he farmed years ago, some hours away from Manila. And now she confesses the dead man's sin, a secret she might have kept in his life but, now, divulges after his death.

"Who was she? The other woman?" Joshua, the younger of her sons, asks.

"I don't know," she lies.

"How long did it last?"

"A few months, maybe less."

"When did it happen?"

"When he first came to the States. Before we arrived."

"We were children then." Joshua turns to his older brother. "We were children."

"I don't have anything to say." Paul glares back.

"Of course you don't," Joshua says. "You're just like him."

When Paul decided to go to college out of state, Melinda knew he wouldn't succeed. A mother always knows her children. But Mickey encouraged him, as if in doing so he could live vicariously through his son, running away from home and from her. Sure enough, Paul flunked out at the end of his first semester, so he came back home, transferred to a local city school, and—as Melinda always knew when she got it her way—all was right. It was only later that they found out why Paul had failed all his classes, when his girlfriend from Ohio came looking for him at their apartment. Melinda hadn't known everything after all. Not about her sons, and not about her husband. All had not been right.

"We've kept our secrets throughout the years," Melinda says. "From each other and from the two of you. But your father wanted me to tell you when the time was right." She is lying again.

"When the time was right?" Joshua says.

"You know your father."

"Aren't you angry, Ma?"

"He's dead," Paul says. He takes a swig from his bottle of Red Horse beer. "What's there to be angry about?"

"Ma?" Joshua presses.

Melinda watches her son's eyes glisten, noticing how she hasn't expressed the same lament nor shed the same tears of fervor. It must be hard for him, the baby of the family, to find out his father wasn't perfect. But she knew she had to tell them about it. If not as a cautionary tale for the men they would grow up to be, then for some sense of relief that she would not bear the burden of his secret alone. Melinda knew Mickey wasn't perfect; she always held herself above him, morally, religiously. "You could have done better," her family had told her. But she was convinced it was love, and if it had faded long ago, God obligated her to be with him till death do them part. Now he is dead.

"Your brother is right," she says. "There's no point in being angry at a dead man."

The waitress comes around with their food. She is in her early twenties, has an hourglass figure, and keeps her dark, brown hair up in a bun. Her hips hit the table, and although she doesn't notice, Melinda catches the boys staring. "Eto na po," the waitress says, almost mockingly. Melinda doesn't take to her false kindness, interrupting their family affairs. She glares at her. "Small plate of pancit," the waitress says. She slides it onto the table, but before her fingers release the plate, Melinda pulls it towards herself, like a child who refuses to share. The waitress ignores her, keeping up her suave bravado. She continues, "Lechon kawali combo." Joshua raises his hand nervously, struggling to keep his eyes on the crispy, brown pork cubes rather than her cleavage. But as she leans over with the last plate, Paul doesn't avoid the sight. "At dinuguan combo," she says, "Para kay gwapo." She hands it to Paul, whose hand glides over hers in the exchange.

"Salamat," Paul says. He adds under his breath, "*Maganda*."

The waitress blushes before walking away, still swaying her hips. She must be so impressed with her son's butchered Filipino pronunciation, Melinda thinks to herself. Paul's eyes linger until she disappears behind the bar and through the kitchen doors. He is just like his father.

"Eat your food before it gets cold," Melinda says.

She twists her plastic fork into her pancit, a swirl of soy-soaked noodles and stir-fried vegetables. Joshua pokes his fork into the pork, biting into it skin first, crackling like bone. Paul takes a spoon into the Styrofoam cup full of dinuguan, pouring half of the pork blood stew over his plate of rice. A feast fit for a funeral.

★

During Mickey's final days in the hospital, Melinda would feed her husband spoonfuls of arroz caldo. She blew on it to cool, the way she used to feed her infant sons, and wiped his drool away with a handkerchief. When they were in high school, Mickey had large arms she used to cling to, a slab of muscle and flesh over a stalky physique. He was a farm boy and he had inherited a farmer's body. She threw herself at him, leaped into his embrace, knowing that Mickey would stand still, resolute, always there to catch her. Now his body was giving up; the cancer had done its job. If she pressed too hard on his arm, even merely resting her head, Mickey would wince in pain. Too many years away from his land and from carrying bags of rice and rearing the carabao, not enough conditioning to maintain his physique. His body never acclimated to America, and now it had taken its toll. He was only forty years old—Melinda knew he was too young to die. Their sons had yet to marry, had yet to give them grandchildren. Outside the window of the hospital, Melinda could see the lush spring greenery of a park. She couldn't help but think of scripture and the ironic fate of Moses, who set his eyes on the Promised

143

Land but never made it. It was Mickey, after all, who had led them to America.

Mickey was no prophet, and he was far from a saint. On his death bed, he asked the doctor, the priest, and his sons to leave the room. This confession was between him and Melinda alone. "I was unfaithful," he said outright. He was blunt and unwavering, even as his voice quelled to a weak whisper. "I'm sorry, Melinda."

"Was it that waitress?"

Melinda had met her when she and the boys first arrived and lived with Mickey. She remembered her name: Laurel, a Filipina waitress whom he had met at a café. She was young, had married an American stationed in Manila who brought her back to the States. Laurel wanted to be an actress on Broadway and sought to become the next Lea Salonga. Melinda had dreamt of the same before they had the boys. She only met Laurel that one time, at a party to commemorate their coming to America. Laurel came alone, without her husband. Melinda had suspicions but immediately dismissed her feelings as mere jealousy. *Mickey could never.* But he could, and he did.

"It was Laurel," Melinda said it for her husband. "The other woman."

"Don't tell the boys," Mickey said. "They shouldn't have to know."

She nodded, a courtesy rather than a promise. He passed away that night.

★

"Come on," Paul says to Joshua. The brothers get up from their seats and walk over to one of the pool tables, leaving pieces of pork and strands of noodles on their plates, flies swirling over and satisfied with the leftovers. Melinda looks to the kitchen doors, waving a hand. She can see the waitress through the small window. The waitress sees Melinda wave but ignores her and laughs instead, perhaps to the other workers in the kitchen. "Nakakainis," she says under a breath. "No tip for you." She swats the flies away and takes up their plates herself, walking towards the trash bin, which is just by the doors to the restaurant's back alley. She walks through them.

Melinda knows this place. She and Mickey used to come here with their high school friends. Mickey, whose cousin had worked at the bar back then, was able to grab some cans of San Miguel for them and their friends. At night, they sat around on milk crates, drinking and exchanging the latest tsismis: "Did you hear Jordan's sister is dating Mika's cousin? No? They were caught making out by the basketball courts. Did you hear Maribel broke up with Anthony? She's moving to Manila for university and leaving him behind." There was always someone from someone else's family, breaking up, making up, and doing it all over again. Back then, and even now, television and radio reception was scarce in their little valley town, so instead of teleseryes and celebrity talk shows, they filled their lives with stories about each other. Melinda would laugh at their stories, those innocent teenagers who had no idea what love was. As she sat in Mickey's lap, those farmer arms around her, Melinda knew what they had was real. Now she thinks how naïve she was, too. How easy it is to believe in fairytales when you come from a world so small. For a moment she understands Mickey and his fascination with that distant land of America.

"Oh," a man says beside her, interrupting her train of thought and memory. He had just walked out the back door with a lighter and cigarette already in hand. He hesitates to light the cylinder. "Excuse me, Miss."

"It's okay," she says, unbothered.

He lights a flame for his cigarette and, retrieving a box of Marlboros from a pocket, offers one to Melinda. "Sigarilyo?"

She had given up smoking for some years when Paul and Joshua were born, but as they grew older and spent more time out of the house than in, Melinda would sometimes open a window and steal one. Mickey would come home from work, smell the smoke, and ask her for one too. They'd spend the evening together in silence, a touch and kiss here and there, watching their smoke mix with the hazy mists of the city outside their window. When Mickey was first diagnosed with cancer, Melinda wondered why it had caught up to him and not her. But after Mickey's confession of infidelity, she believed the sin had more to do with it than the carcinogens.

She accepts the stranger's offer.

"Thanks." As he comes close to light her cigarette, Melinda gets a clearer view of his face. He has dark brown skin, the kind one inherits and grows into, fortified by years of working in the sun. He has patches of hair across his chin and cheeks, yet the effect is more manly than adolescent. She smells his breath tinged with smoke and beer. With his palms cupped around her cigarette and his large arms curled over, Melinda notices how much he reminds her of her husband. He is healthy, perhaps in his prime, and—unlike her husband—he is alive. The resemblance is merely coincidental, Melinda thinks to herself. "Thank you again," she says.

They spend some moments in silence, taking turns breathing in and letting out smoke. In the distance, Melinda sees some storm clouds forming over the mountain range. There's a flash of lightning, yet its thunder hits softly. The storm is headed towards them.

"You're not from around here, huh," the stranger says. "Manila?"

"I grew up *here*, actually," she answers. "But I've since moved to the States."

"Sorry I assumed," he says. "So, you're a balikbayan."

Melinda never thought she would be labeled as such. Growing up, she had cousins who visited from Europe and America. Her parents made her befriend them, but she never saw them as family. They were too different—with their Western accents and butchered Tagalog, much like her sons have now. But is she too different as well? Did she no longer blend in with her fellow countrymen, not even in her hometown?

"Do you still speak Ilocano?" The stranger, who had been speaking with Melinda in Tagalog, switches to their local dialect.

"Of course," Melinda responds, matching his mother tongue. "How could I forget my own language?"

"Either you're quite convincing, or you truly are from here." He says this as if she had passed a test, which offends Melinda only a little as she takes comfort in knowing her tongue hasn't failed her. "There are many balikbayans who come here and forget Ilocano. Even the OFWs who live here prefer to speak English," he scoffs.

She and Mickey had considered retiring in the Philippines, like the other Overseas Filipino Workers who chased their dreams to America and back. There were already quite a few OFWs in town while they were growing up. When she accompanied her parents to the wet market, they pointed them out like paparazzi. They always wore luxury name brands like Coach or Michael Kors, American trademarks and their claim to local celebrity. They weren't necessarily actors or models. They were doctors and teachers, architects and engineers—normal jobs in the States. But in their home province, OFWs were anything but normal. They were the lucky ones who made it out with nothing and came back with everything.

The stranger continues, "They've built their mansions along Bonifacio. Have you seen that street? Block after block, mansion after mansion. All in pink and blue colors. Gated, of course. That's what American money can get you here."

"Then I don't have American money."

"Well, you're still young. There's still time."

"I think I'm older than you," she presses him. He must be at least a decade younger than she.

"Really? I couldn't tell." He smiles with his cigarette gritted between his teeth, which makes her blush, surprisingly.

His flirtation catches Melinda off guard. Did he not see the wrinkles around her eyes, the age setting into her temples? Sure, she had put on makeup for Mickey's funeral, but that was hours ago and she must have sweated it off by now. He must have mistaken her sleek, black funeral dress for a cocktail one.

"What brings you back?" he asks. "A boyfriend?"

149

A husband, she answers in thought. Should she tell him the truth, that she had come back to bury her dead husband?

"Family," she says instead. "A funeral," which isn't a lie at all.

"Shet." The black dress clicks for him. "I'm sorry."

Melinda nods as she lets some smoke touch the back of her throat. Wary that the stranger would continue to question her, she asks him, "What are you doing here?"

"I'm also a balikbayan of sorts," he answers. "Of this town, not the country. I drive a truck. I'm on my way to Baguio with a shipment of towels and bed sheets. But I grew up here too, and I also don't have American money. I've left many times, but I always make sure to return to my roots."

"And do you always talk up every woman you find on these trips?"

"Only the beautiful ones," he answers, then takes one last hit of his cigarette.

It's cheesy, cliché, and juvenile, but Melinda can't help but feel young again. He talks the way Mickey had talked all those years ago, smooth yet always affectionate. Years into their marriage, most of it spent in the States, Mickey's suggestive advances dwindled. This stranger, however, seems to have kept his cool charm and allure. He drops the blunt end of his cigarette and presses it into the ground with his shoe.

"Another one?" He takes one for himself but waits for her answer before replacing the Marlboros in his pocket.

Her cigarette, too, is near its end. She finishes it off with a long breath and puts it out on the ground, mimicking the stranger's confidence. She grabs another one from the box, accepting his offer. The stranger comes close again and wraps an arm over hers to get to her cigarette, which Melinda holds still between her lips. She's nervous, but not uncomfortable. When he lights the flame, she stares straight into his dark brown eyes. If he is indeed her husband, by some supernatural circumstance, she takes it as a second chance—Mickey's repentance for infidelity. But if he isn't the same man she had married, well, it's a second chance for her—not at love, perhaps, but at some romance and fun. She had kept up her end of their vows, till death do us part. Unlike Mickey, she was faithful all along. She deserves, at least, some compensation for his breach of contract. So, just as the stranger finishes lighting her cigarette and begins to pull away, Melinda presses herself against him, replacing the cigarette between her lips with his lips. He doesn't pull away.

It begins to drizzle around them. But it doesn't break the spell the stranger has on Melinda. She lets herself enjoy him, his smoky breath against her neck, his brawny arms around her. A flash of lightning and its subsequent thunder breaks their scene. When they pull away, they set their eyes to the ground. They hadn't noticed how hard the rain was falling, so much so their shoes are nearly covered in water. They look back up, their eyes meet. They blush, knowing that they aren't quite finished with each other yet. So Melinda leads him back inside, turning immediately into the bathroom, avoiding being seen by the others and her sons. She locks the door behind them.

★

The last time she and Mickey had made love was right after his diagnosis. He had been coughing up phlegm for months, though he had no cold nor flu. It was Melinda who finally persuaded him to visit the doctor. He held onto his pride, even when it came to his health. By the time he made the appointment, it was too late. "Lung cancer," the doctor said. "Severe," he stressed. When they got home to their apartment—their sons still out in the city—Mickey retrieved a pack of cigarettes for them to smoke, as if they could easily go back to their evening routine.

"No, Mickey," Melinda ordered him.

"Last pack," he said. "Let me enjoy this."

"I'm serious, Mickey." She tried to grab the box, but his grip was still too strong. She tried repeatedly to take the cigarettes from him, chasing him around their little apartment. They were like their younger selves again, before Mickey's cancer got the best of him, before it began to put a strain on their marriage. Their romance had been petering out for some years, which made Mickey's newfound vitality an anomaly. But with the news of his cancer, of his body deteriorating in every day he lived, how else could he react? This was one of the last times she saw her husband so active. "Puwes," she said. "Your lungs are going to give out sooner or later."

"Don't say that," he said.

"You heard the doctor. Severe lung cancer."

"Fine," he said, surrendering the cigarettes to her.

After throwing them into the trash bin, she joined Mickey on the couch. He was already lying down, his demeanor no longer childlike. He was thinking, seriously now, about the diagnosis. Melinda rested her head against his chest and let his arms fall around her. She could hear his heavy breathing—how did she not see this coming? She thought about how her life would be without him.

"How are we going to tell the boys?"

"When the time is right," he assured her. The time was never right. Two weeks after his first round of chemotherapy, the boys caught on to his illness, his hair falling out in clumps onto the floor. But he only wanted to protect them from the truth, that they might have to lose their father. Even in his failings as a husband, Melinda knew he did his best for Paul and Joshua. This couldn't have been the life he envisioned when he dreamt up America. For Melinda, this—like moving halfway across the world—had never been in her plans. But neither was having to forgive her husband for an affair.

That evening of his diagnosis was the last time Melinda saw his body in its glory, before he shed his farmer's body for a corpse's eight months later. Mickey had a birthmark on his back, a white smudge against his brown skin. When she kissed it, Mickey would laugh and giggle, tickled by her lips.

Now, as she and the stranger wind down in the bathroom, Melinda finds no such birthmark. His back is bare, yet still just as muscular. *This is not your husband*, she assures herself. *This is not his ghost*. When they finish, she picks herself up off of him. She pulls her black dress down over her legs.

"Wait five minutes before you leave," she tells him.

"Yes, Miss." He buttons up his shirt and picks up his pants on the floor. "How long are you in town?"

"I leave for the States tomorrow." She can see the disappointment on his face, however charming.

"Will I see you again?"

"Maybe when I come back with real American money. You'll find me in my mansion on Bonifacio," she jokes. She wonders if she would want to come back years later without Mickey by her side, and how lonely it would be to have a mansion all to herself. Her sons would surely be settled and stable in the States by then, their futures secured. But what would become of her? Melinda continues, "Until then, you'll have the other women on your trips."

"But they won't be you." He's still got his cool, which makes Melinda smile. But she knows she can't stay. Her sons must be wondering where she's been all this time. He adds, "Can I at least have your name?"

"Five minutes," she reminds the stranger. She walks out of the bathroom and leaves him in the stall.

★

Melinda rushes back into the saloon, finding her sons on either side of the waitress that served them. Paul leans against the pool table and steals her attention. She's laughing, entertaining him, leaning into him with her hips. Joshua's having trouble keeping up with them, awkwardly hanging his head over the waitress's shoulder.

"Let's go." Melinda takes both her sons by their arms. Paul keeps telling her to wait, but she pulls him away from the waitress anyway. "Leave her."

"I didn't even get her number," Paul says.

"You could barely understand her Tagalog," Joshua says. "Get over yourself."

"And you could have done better?" Paul says. "You wouldn't have been able to get anything in with her, not even a word."

"Shut up, you two."

The boys listen.

Melinda walks to the bar and, without counting, leaves some pesos for the bill. She hears the waitress calling after her in Tagalog, "Ina, make sure to leave a big tip for your sons." The waitress laughs to herself. She reminds Melinda of Mickey's lover—Laurel, the other woman who had worked her husband so many years ago. "Puta," Melinda curses under her breath.

She finds her reflection in the mirror behind the liquor counter, her lipstick smudged down her chin. She wipes it off with the side of her hand.

As she leads her sons to the exit, one of the lonely men at the bar moves to the pool table and tries his shot with the waitress. Melinda pushes her sons through the doors, keeping their eyes forward.

Outside, the rain's already begun to amass, the street no longer a street but a shallow stream. There are others leaving from the neighboring shops of the truck-stop plaza and making the trek towards a jeepney. They've rolled up their jeans to their knees and hold plastic bags over their heads. "We can make it," Melinda tells her sons. And together they sprint towards the jeepney, bathed in rain, and find the last seats in the back.

As the jeepney pulls away from the plaza, Melinda eyes the stranger walking out into the rain. He looks around the parking lot, searching for her, but she avoids his sight. As they drive off onto the road, the man gives up his search, hanging his head, just as dour as the weather.

As she watches her husband's doppelganger return to the saloon, she wonders if her true husband would find out about her brief tryst. Even as they've returned him to Philippine soil, would he find his way out of the dirt, walk through airport security, and follow them home to their apartment seeking revenge? Would she find him standing there, confronting her with her own infidelity? *No*, she answers herself. No—they were even. It's all fair game now that she is a widow. Mickey would have easily done the same had it been the other way around. He had done so in life when they were married. She would not let Mickey haunt her when they go back to the States.

Melinda wipes the rain off her face and turns her stare towards her sons. They stare back at their mother, still her children as they've always been, waiting for her words to reassure them that everything was going to be okay. Yet she also sees their father in their eyes. Despite her wish to leave Mickey behind in the Philippines, she realizes that her sons have inherited his ghost. She wonders when they will eventually find their own wives—surely American ones—when she will no longer be the only woman in their lives. Their time will come, Melinda thinks to herself, and so will hers—when her love, again, would be betrayed...when she, again, would not be enough.

TONG, TONG, TONG

We were lying naked in a Manila hotel room, a
few hours after the flight. The room smelled of
generic lavender, and the dimly lit modern light
fixtures kept the darkness at bay. The walls, once
white, had yellowed with age and were bordered
by brown, like an old colonial home from the
distant Spanish past, now cooled by the air conditioning. In the distance outside, the Pacific waves
gently crashed against the night. Tara leaned her
head into me and whispered a tune, *tong, tong,
tong, tong*...

"It's about a crab," Tara said. A simple nursery
rhyme. Her hand mimicked the motions of a crustacean crawling up my arm, each finger a tiny
leg stepping to the distinct beat...*pakitong-kitong*.
"Big, delicious, but tricky to catch," she continued.
The crab lunged from my shoulder, pinching my
earlobe. "It bites."

"I don't remember that one," I said, wincing.
I filed through childhood memories, searching
for that crab, trying to remember what it was like
before my parents whisked me away to the States.
The only nursery rhyme that came to mind was

159

about a hut made of bamboo and leaves. I had already forgotten the lyrics.

"That's a different one," Tara said, caressing my ear between a finger and thumb. The crab was no longer a crab but her smooth, delicate hand. "You're too American now," she teased in Tagalog, "Amerikano."

This was my first visit to the Philippines since my parents died—my father in a car crash, followed shortly by my mother from a heart attack. My mother always insisted on being buried in the same cemetery as her relatives in the Philippines. "We have a whole plot all to ourselves," she would brag as if tombstones were trophies, a row of them on public display. My father didn't have a grave in mind, so he ended up in a small, additional lot alongside my mother's family. He was always that way, so caught up in appeasing his wife's wishes that he never got his own. He would say, "A happy wife, a happy life." I wondered if it was the same for the two of them in the afterlife— whether either of them were happy, or if happiness was even possible. Their funerals were five years ago, the last time I had been in my home country. Before that, my last time in the Philippines was when I was two, leaving for the States with vague memories and mistranslated nursery rhymes. I was too American now, Tara was right. I didn't remember much at all.

★

I was in Manila for the wedding of William and Sophia, my friends from college. Growing up, I didn't think much of the Philippines since I left, not until I met them. Sophia was an international student from the Philippines who came to our university in her junior year. There weren't many Filipinos on campus, and the few often hung around in cliques. Perhaps I could have been part of that little Pinoy community, having been approached to attend weekly meetings involving Filipino food, but I declined. I got enough lumpia from my parents when they visited, and my tastes leaned more towards cheeseburgers and fries than dinuguan. Sophia must have been looking for that community, which was how we first met.

"You're Filipino?" she asked, approaching me in the quad. But to her disappointment, I wasn't much of one. While the Filipino cliques often had potluck dinners—kamayan nights—and line dances, I was either with William playing Call of Duty or watching some five-dollar matinee at the downtown theater. When I told her my major was in art history, her disappointment continued in questions. "Why not an engineer?"—her brother was an engineer in the Philippines. "Why not a nurse?"—she was pursuing a nursing degree. She sounded like my parents. I had been a biology major like William, with plans to pursue a medical career. Then I saw how all the other Filipinos, no matter how few, were in the same classes. I couldn't quite explain my aversion to joining them, but I resisted any aspect that could have pigeonholed me as one of them, even if it meant my exclusion. I refused to be a stereotype. So I switched my major to art and never looked back.

It was William who gravitated towards Sophia. When I introduced her to William, she was already lost in his all-American-ness. He was as white as they came, with a squared jaw and freckles that came out in the summer. His voice seemed stuck in that slightly-after-puberty stage, like a teenager posing as a grown-up. They said it was love at first sight, and I believed it was true. William was the one who joined her at those Friday night meetings full of Filipino food and karaoke. Though they invited me, I still refused, citing some art project that needed to be done. But I watched their romance blossom. By the spring semester of junior year, they were together seriously. Their marriage, it seemed, was always inevitable.

In between semesters, I invited them to my home, which was a four-hour drive from the college. My parents didn't visit me on campus, so I figured I would introduce them to William and Sophia. Almost instantly, my parents grew fond of William, extending an invitation for all future family gatherings. They loved Sophia, too. Unlike me, she kept her Tagalog tongue and even spoke Ilocano, the language my father spoke from his province. My parents teased me, of course, using William as an example. "See? If you were a doctor, you would already have a girlfriend." A *Filipino* girlfriend, they insinuated.

The three of us remained close until the end of college. When William went to medical school and Sophia returned to the Philippines as a nurse, they kept a long-distance relationship. Meanwhile, I grew distant from them. I found work as an art instructor at a community college near my parents. I thought it best to live with them until I could afford somewhere better. When they asked about William and Sophia, I told them how well they were doing in their careers. All the while, they reminded me of how I could have been just like them. By the time I felt like it was the right time to reach out to them and plan a reunion, life had other plans. Then came the car accident that took my father's life, and then my mother's heart attack. At the time, William was preoccupied with his residency. I also decided not to tell Sophia. I didn't doubt that she would have come as a friend to the funerals, but I felt it had been too long since our college days. Perhaps I should have told them about their deaths sooner, considering how they were practically family according to my parents.

But now, we three would be back together in Manila of all places. I was to be William's best man. "We wouldn't be together if it wasn't for you," William had told me over the phone. His voice hadn't changed since college; it was like we never left. Apart from my parents, William and Sophia had been the closest people in my life, so I agreed to be William's best man.

*

As I lay next to Tara, I had more on my mind than William and Sophia's wedding. While I found them attractive, I was never infatuated with Filipino women, an immature fear that one might have been a distant relative. Even though my parents wanted me to find a girl like Sophia, I always found it strange when, standing on the subway, any given Filipino would stare at me until I noticed, and they would nod at me, gesturing, *You are one of us.* I'd smile reluctantly, then turn the other way. Now, I found myself in bed with Tara, the only intimacy I've shared with another Filipino, as if being in the homeland gave me permission and reassurance—Tara's touch telling me, *You are one of us.*

On the plane, her face was much paler, under layers of powder and pigments, a hint of blush across her cheeks. She must have shared the same routine with the other flight attendants, whose faces hid the same tropical traces. Even in sound, their voices lost the authority of strong consonants and quick syllables, the authority of my parents' mother tongue, scolding, commanding. They spoke in soft gestures instead: sir, miss, please.

"Sir," Tara had said, leaning into my aisle seat, "Coffee or tea?"

"Coffee," I replied. I was sketching a baby in the aisle across from me, the mother lulling the plump infant in her arms to sleep. Tara eyed my sketchbook as she poured, careful not to spill. Then her eyes met mine, a blip in her uniformed performance. We smiled. "Thanks," I said as she handed me the hot drink. Then she returned to her routine, "Coffee or tea?" right down the aisle of the plane.

When the flight landed and all the baggage was retrieved, we found each other waiting for a cab outside the terminal. Children ran to greet their aunts and uncles; significant others embraced for too long. Tara had a few bags, including a balikbayan box. When I went to help her load her things into a taxi van, she tried handing me a couple of bills—first in pesos then in dollars.

"At least let me share the cab with you," she offered.

I didn't have much, just a carry-on roller. Unlike her, I had no need for a balikbayan box, no family waiting for presents or supplies. I looked back at the horde of other arrivals, clamoring over taxis to haul themselves and their belongings to waiting loved ones. Then Tara mentioned her destination, and we realized we were staying at the same hotel.

"Wait," I said, grabbing the taxicab door before she could close it. "Okay, I accept the offer."

I didn't expect the ride to take so long. But as the afternoon sunlight gradually turned to evening, and the cab had only moved a few miles, I couldn't help but feel the tense air between Tara and me—the hot, tropical humidity didn't help either. "There's an accident on the expressway," the driver explained, cutting through the silence. Tara and I exchanged looks. She said something in Tagalog that I couldn't quite make out, maybe something about taking a shortcut or even the lack of air-conditioning in the car. The driver merely responded, "Sorry, mam. Hindi po puede."

"Your art is beautiful," she said to me. I had taken out my sketchbook and began finishing the piece I started on the plane, which was shaping up to be an in-flight rendition of the Madonna and child.

"Salamat," I attempted to thank her in Tagalog, which was met by her smirk. Despite the heat, I could also feel my cheeks go warm.

"I wanted to be an artist, too," Tara added.

"Let me guess, your parents said you couldn't."

"Actually, they didn't really care," she explained. "One of the perks of being the youngest. The problem was that I wasn't a very good artist."

I handed her my sketchbook and pencil. Tara raised an eyebrow.

"Prove it," I said. "Draw me."

After a moment of hesitation, she accepted the challenge. She took her time, glancing between my face and the blank page. I didn't watch what she was actually putting down on the paper. As her subject, I kept still, which was easy considering how slow the traffic moved. While she was focusing on me, I kept my stare on her fingers, which moved with the pencil in lines and circles, scribbling out shapes that didn't satisfy her. When she finally handed the sketchbook back to me, I laughed. She had merely drawn a smiley face. "See? Not very good."

That was enough to cut the tension.

We continued to talk throughout the ride. Tara spoke about the cities she'd visited: Rio de Janeiro, Abu Dhabi, Moscow. She demonstrated her limited proficiency in foreign languages, such as French and Korean. Then her speech eventually settled between English and Tagalog, her accent growing harder and more demanding. As she spoke, she took a face wipe from her purse and took off her makeup. She undid her hair and let it fall to her shoulders. By the time we arrived at the hotel and reached our room, Tara was almost unrecognizable as the flight attendant I had met some hours before. Despite all the places she'd been to, there was still her true Filipino self underneath her uniform and accents. I felt no such change in myself.

Perhaps it was finally having the freedom to move after spending hours in that taxi or the immediate relief of the air conditioning in the hotel room that led us immediately to bed, one touch after the other. Then came the song, *Tong, tong, tong, tong, pakitong-kitong.*

"We used to sing that song every day, ever since we learned it at school," she continued. "There were five of us, can you imagine? Going around the house shouting *tong, tong, tong, tong*"— her accent rang true, her tongue determined each note—"then we'd change to *ting, ting, ting, ting.* I don't know how my parents managed."

My parents, who only had me, managed well. My father was a dentist and my mother taught kindergarten. I got good grades in school, and never got into trouble. I was the model immigrant child and, after seventeen years, a citizen. But when my parents passed away, I wondered how I would manage without them.

On the other hand, Tara lived her childhood in the Philippines. She narrated her memories, which were mostly made up of early mornings before the sun rose over Manila. "Mama didn't need to raise her voice," she said. Instead, she recalled how her mother would start up a frying pan on the stove and throw in a handful of pusit and danggit. The pungent, salty smell of dried squid and fish was enough to wake anyone from the deepest sleep. Tara continued, "I never got used to it. It was gross, which was practical. It made me want to shower and get dressed right away." She inhaled the bedsheets for a moment, taking in the lavender. "My school uniform smelled much better."

"Now look at you. You get to travel the world," I said. Was her life any different as a flight attendant, waking up at sporadic times and slipping into a newly washed and ironed uniform? Whenever she was back in the Philippines, did her mother still iron and press her uniform before she left for a flight? "And you get to come back," I added.

"My mother's sick," she said. "The doctor told my siblings she has a few months left. They caught the cancer too late." She went back to the song, *tong, tong, tong*...But her hand looked numb, no longer the crustacean with claws. She was still leaning into me, but her eyes were fixed on the ceiling, a beige canvas in the faint light. What was she drawing in her mind? "The crab bites back," she concluded.

I let her drift to sleep. Her breathing matched the waves outside, gently advancing and receding. I reached for a pencil from my bag, then began to draw her. The moonlight seeped through the window and clung to her silhouette, the contours of her body forming a clear edge. She held her position, the cotton sheets rising and falling with her body. While my body had yet to adjust to the time and place, Tara slept just fine.

I didn't want to admit it. But when William and Sophia paired off in college, I became the odd one out. When I lost my parents, the feeling was harder to ignore. I was lonely. I had been for a long time.

⋆

In the morning, Tara had to leave for Pangasinan. She arranged for another van to pick her up from the hotel, but this time she would share it with other strangers looking to make the five-hour journey through winding roads and the Filipino countryside if the Manila traffic didn't hold them back. Meanwhile, I had to get ready for the wedding.

When the sky outside awoke with a glimmer of pink and orange, I got out of bed and unzipped my carry-on. The barong was only mildly crumpled, but the black dress pants had developed their own topography. I could hear my mother's voice in the back of my mind, nagging me. "Ang lukot lukot," she would say, pointing out the noticeable creases in the fabric. "You should have had it dry-cleaned!" But there was no time for the dry cleaners now, and I could no longer wish for my mother to stop nagging me.

"Ang lukot." This time I heard it for real. Tara had woken up. "What's that for?"

"A wedding," I said.

"Wow! Bongga bongga," Tara teased. "I didn't know I was the other woman."

"You're not," I said, embarrassed. "It's for a friend's wedding."

She got up from bed, looking over my shoulder and pointing out the crumpled-up barong and pants. I let her head rest in the crevice between my neck and shoulder. "Steam should help with those creases," she said. So I hung the outfit on a hanger and hooked it behind the bathroom door, and then we both slipped into a hot shower. When we got out, she helped me dress. I thought of my mother on the night of college graduation, making sure my tie was centered along the line of buttons on my white shirt. Tara buttoned the collar up to my neck—her fingers felt like the pinch of a little crab.

"Tong, tong, tong," I attempted to sing, my muddled, too-American mouth struggling to recall the words.

"Needs work," she teased.

"I'll get it right next time," I said, not knowing if there would be a next time.

Before I left, I walked her out to the van. She didn't have her airline uniform on, just a red tank top over blue jeans. Her face was free of makeup, her deep brown skin glistening in the morning sun. Just as I did at the airport, I helped her carry her belongings to the van. I thought of convincing her to stay by inviting her as my plus-one, even though I'd already checked off a single RSVP months ago. But her mother was waiting for her arrival, and I couldn't take that away from her, not while they still had each other. Instead, I presented her with the sketch I had drawn of her the night before.

"You keep it," Tara insisted. She asked for a pencil and wrote a phone number on its back. "So you can find me when we're back in New York." She kissed me on the cheek and, before jumping into the van, pinched my ear with her hand, the crab. I watched the van drive out of the parking lot and onto the street, alongside jeepneys, tricycles, and motorcycles—the steady stream of urban Manila—and waved goodbye.

*

The wedding took place in an old Catholic church in a section of Manila called Intramuros, the colonial headquarters of the Spanish way back when. Intramuros was a walled city, whose buildings all bore the same brown and yellow bricks. Its streets were tight, not made for two-way traffic, especially not for a limo. The ceremony itself was as expected. Back in New York, my parents had dragged me to other weddings of titos and titas—some true blood relatives but most just their colleagues and friends. William and Sophia's wedding was three hours of mostly standing. The orchestral songs were dramatic enough to make the colonial barebones of the church tremble. For a while, I moved my mouth to keep up with the Tagalog songs and readings, but I eventually surrendered to silence, chiming in only for the occasional "Amen." As the best man, I had to stand in front of everyone, pretending my feet weren't blistering in my dress shoes.

The reported temperature was ninety degrees, but it was amplified by the hundred or so attending the ceremony, and the church wasn't made for air conditioning. The electric fans did their best. Sweat seeped through my barong—the last time I wore one was for my parents' funeral. The other men, too, wore the traditional shirt—a thin, see-through fabric with flowery designs. In colonial times, Spanish officers forced Filipinos to wear it because of its transparent fabric, which allowed them to ensure no daggers or weapons were hidden beneath. But now, a whole church congregation had men wearing barongs, right in the capital of Spanish colonial rule. Even William.

"A happy wife, a happy life," I echoed my father in my best man's speech at the reception. In the cooler, air-conditioned banquet hall, I felt more comfortable.

"You know," William said, "you might take that advice sometime soon."

"I've been talking you up with all of my cousins," Sophia said. She gestured to a table full of young women. A few giggled as they caught us eyeing them. She continued, "Any of them would be lucky to have you."

"I'll take my chances back in the States," I said. I decided to withhold Tara from them. I kept my sketch of her in my pocket, like some kind of totem or lucky charm. If I told them about Tara, if I revealed our secret little tryst, would I somehow ruin my chances of finding her again? I would wait until we rendezvoused in New York, whenever that would be.

"If I were you," Sophia added, "I wouldn't close the door on women around here. They're all looking for some handsome American to whisk them away."

"Just take a look at Sophia," William joked. "Now she's my wife." They both laughed. I should have been happy for them, and by all appearances I was, laughing uncomfortably.

Fortunately, the DJ started the music and called everyone to the dance floor. The opening notes of Earth, Wind, & Fire's "September" beckoned everyone out of their seats.

"I actually know this fucking line dance," William said.

He met Sophia at the front of the dance floor, and behind them were five rows of miscellaneous Filipinos from Sophia's side and some of William's white family members who struggled to mimic the movements. It was an awful sight, but for everyone else, it must have been fun. I approached the open bar, took a double shot of rum, and did my best on the dance floor. I also knew the steps to "September" like a good Filipino. I could at least be one, if only for a dance number.

★

I don't remember much after the dancing and the spinning of it all—the echoing of ABBA's "Dancing Queen" reverberating through the banquet hall. When William and Sophia found me an hour after the reception, I was outside on the beach in a drunken, sandy stupor. They found me with my face thrust into the sand, the back of my neck burnt red, and my shoes filled with ocean water from Manila Bay. I was mumbling and slurring my words, refusing to wake up from an apparent dream. Crabs had scurried all over me, so they called over some paramedics to pry the pincers off my arms and legs. William and Sophia helped me back to the hotel with patches of Band-Aids covering the pricks all over my body.

"You kept calling out to Tara," William said, "in between some song."

"Tong—uh—pa-ki-tong—uh—ki-tong," Sophia sang clumsily, mocking what had been my drunken rendition. "I didn't think you'd know it. Did Tara teach you that?"

"And who the hell is Tara? Is that one of your cousins?" William asked his now wife.

"None of mine," Sophia answered. "Did you mean Cara? I didn't see her as your type."

Still in a drunken haze, I shook my head.

"If you've been seeing someone, then you have to tell us," they egged on. "Who's Tara?"

I reached into my pocket for her picture—the sketch I had drawn of Tara with her phone number on it. But when I took the picture out, it unfolded like a wilting salad. I looked at what remained of my drawing—the lead was all streaks and smudges on the sodden piece of paper. I turned it over to find that her phone number was also lost to the ocean.

"Who's Tara?" they repeated.

"Just some girl," I said. I wanted to say she was someone special, to tell them I had found someone too. But I couldn't, not when I had lost the only trace of her.

When their wedding had all wrapped up and I returned to New York alone, I realized that letting her go was for the best. Even though I knew the chances were nearly impossible, I held on to the slight hope that Tara might have been on the same flight back. But the crew was entirely new. Instead, I imagined her with her siblings, crouched next to their ailing mother in bed in her final moments. Tara was where she needed to be—where she belonged. Me? I was Amerikano, like she had said. Still, I never did get that damn nursery rhyme out of my head.

SINIGANG

I thought I saw you at the grocery store, pushing
a shopping cart through the ethnic food aisle. You
were looking for a packet of seasoning, the one
you'd mix into a pot of boiling water, simmering
with braised pork and vegetables. Tamarind soup,
sinigang. In winter you made a pot every other
night, its warm, sour broth a cure for the New
England cold. "We weren't made for this," you
told me, a child shivering from the frigid air and
excitement of first-time snow. "Filipinos don't
belong in the snow." You served me a bowl of
sinigang over rice, steam rising over white, fluffy
flakes. I spooned the broth and rice over each
other, like a child still playing in the frost. I gulped
it down with a grimace, sucking in my cheeks as
the sour struck my tongue. You reminded me that
there were only two seasons in the Philippines,
rainy and dry. You reminded me how much you
missed it.

★

I looked for the packet of seasoning at the grocery
store, in the ethnic food aisle, like you told me to.

You had given me a list of ingredients written on the back of an old prayer card: on the front was a picture of Saint Francis. Onions and tomatoes, garlic and ginger, okra or spinach (or some other green vegetable), vinegar, bouillon cubes, and pork belly, which I'd have to cut up into cubes. I went out when it was still snowing. I came back and you were still in bed. Your hair was more gray than brown, and dark spots had begun to form on the surface of your face. "Bring me back home," you said aloud. I didn't respond, too busy chopping up the onions and making sure I wouldn't cry. "Don't bury me here in the snow."

I started with the cubed pork, rendering its fat until the meat browned slightly. Then I let the onions and tomatoes soften in the fat before adding the ginger and garlic. I waited until they were fragrant, until you noticed and yelled "Don't burn it!" from upstairs. I added a few cups of water, the bouillon cubes, and the packet of tamarind soup seasoning. I let it come to a boil, then lowered the heat to a simmer. I added the green vegetables into the pot (I had chosen green beans). When the pork and vegetables were tender, I added a splash of vinegar and seasoned to taste. Still, you complained, "Not enough vinegar. Not enough sour for my sick soul."

★

I thought I saw you at the grocery store in the
ethnic food aisle. I was only just passing by. I
hadn't had sinigang since I left for college, where
my roommates ate only from the frozen food aisle.
All I had to do was preheat the oven for a tray
of frost-covered potato wedges and stone-cold
chicken wings. I'd wait for the timer to sound.
There was football on the television, bottles on
the floor. I don't belong here, I thought. Bring me
back home.

★

I thought I saw you at the grocery store, so I went
up to you to see. It was an old Filipino woman,
short and fragile, and she looked like you. She
had dark spots around her eyes, and her gray hair
wrapped in a ponytail. "Pilipino ka ba?" she asked
me in Tagalog, *Are you Filipino?* She had forgotten
to bring her glasses and had no way of reading
the labels. "Can you help me find the sinigang?"
she asked. I nodded humbly. I took out my wallet
and found the old prayer card of Saint Francis,
then turned it over to the list of ingredients. The
ink had faded, but still I saw your hand. I recognized the brand name and found it on the second
shelf. "Iyan!" the woman said. *That's the one.* I
handed her a few packets, which she slipped into
her shopping cart. She thanked me with a tender

smile and a warm palm on my cheek. I grimaced initially, but her hand didn't flinch. "Mabait ikaw." *You are kind.* Her warm hand like yours, the hand that cooked sinigang and melted away the New England winter.

SLEEPLESS IN AMERICA

I had started sleepwalking again. My wife found me standing outside like a zombie at 2 a.m. in early December. She already knew about my history of sleepwalking, but she never saw it for herself. I told her how the sleepwalking began when I was four years old. My parents sought out a therapist who attributed the symptom to our recent move from the Philippines to the States. "His body is here," the therapist told us, "but his mind is back home." He suggested that my parents get me sleeping pills, which didn't always help. But my condition was mild, each trance only lasting ten minutes. My parents often found me in the bathroom where I relieved myself, at which point I awoke and came back to my senses. I lived a relatively normal life despite the occasional nightspell. But the sleepwalking eventually stopped. Specifically, after my father passed away, I no longer had problems sleeping through the night. That was ten years ago.

Then Layla found me standing on the front lawn, looking down the street as if I were waiting for someone. But no one was coming at this time of night. "Francis, wake up," she said, waving a hand in front of my face. According to her, I merely blinked. She took me back inside. My legs were, fortunately, responsive. She led me to the bathroom where she set me in front of the toilet. She left me there until I awoke to the sound of water splashing. "I don't know why it started again," I told her. We were back in bed. "Actually, maybe, I do. I think it has to do with that old man from the care home—Ignatius. He looks just like my father. And he thinks I'm his son."

★

Ignatius was one of my patients at the Garden of Eden Care Home, one of the assisted living facilities I visited as a physical therapist. The residents were usually concerned with themselves and each other. They were often fighting over seats on the "comfy chair" rather than the hardwood ones. Whenever I pulled them out for a session, I usually called for the one causing the ruckus. They were like children that way, playing musical chairs as if it were life or death—well, for them, understandably so. When I first arrived at Eden, that's exactly what happened.

The director of the home Mrs. Walters, a lengthy woman with short, gray hair who looked like a lovely lady at first sight, guided me through the facility. But when she spoke, her voice sometimes didn't match the movement of her mouth—her noticeable dentures made it so her teeth got in the way of her tongue. She looked like a robot with loose circuits, a malfunction that could have been easily repaired with a wrench. Frankly, I was surprised to find out that Mrs. Walters was the director and not one of the residents.

"This is the living room, where they spend most of their time," she explained. "That's Richard on the couch, sitting next to him is Kerry. Donna likes to sit in Donna's chair—she brought it with her when she moved in (it's imported from Italy). And there is Ignatius, he likes to tinker with the television."

Richard was balding; the only hair on his head was the white around the crown, like snow after an avalanche. He was trading magazines with Kerry. Her hair was worn down and messy, the blonde still blonde, though it could have been dyed. Her lips were pursed, even when she spoke. At the moment, she was annoyed at Richard, who kept grabbing the magazines from her hands before she finished reading them. "Quit it, Richard. Let me take my time," she said.

"You've got all the exciting ones," Richard said. He was talking about the issues of Women's Fitness. Meanwhile, Donna was seated in Donna's chair, sleeping. Her glasses drooped down on her nose; in her lap was a half-finished crocheted blanket.

Then there was Ignatius by the television. When I first applied for the job, the ad boasted the facilities' state of the art resources and amenities. But the television was still a box, something I only saw at garage sales. It sat on top of a cart, like from grammar school days, with cables hooked up to various external machines—a VHS/DVD player, radio, cable box, and speaker. Ignatius was leaning over it, hitting the buttons like a piano player searching for the right key. His brown skin was graying, like old cardboard that was once wet but now dry. But underneath his drooping skin and brown-speckled face, Ignatius reminded me of my father. I saw Papa's flat, brutish nose and thick eyebrows every time I looked into the mirror, and now I saw those same features on Ignatius. He seemed to be what my father would have looked like if he hadn't died years ago. Perhaps he was a long-lost uncle.

"I wouldn't get too attached to them," Mrs. Walters said. Spoken like a true robot. I hoped she would get her dentures attached to the roof of her mouth, but she never did.

After a brief tour of the rest of Eden—which included the kitchen and dining room, mail room, exercise room, and residents' apartments—we returned to the living room to find Richard up in arms because Kerry had stolen his seat. "I go to the bathroom for one second then this skank is there!" Kerry hadn't moved at all.

"I'm sorry about this," Mrs. Walters said, "but this is one of those rare occasions where we do have to intervene." Mrs. Walters got in between Richard and Kerry, who were already throwing curses at each other. Donna was unbothered, still asleep in her assigned Italian chair. In the middle of the chaos, I stood awkwardly next to Ignatius, who was still switching the channels on the television.

"Anak," Ignatius said, gesturing for me to come over. "I can't find TFC."

"I'm sorry," I said. "I don't think they have it here."

"But I am going to miss *Game Ka Na Ba?*. Did your mother pay the bill?"

"I don't know what he means by that," Mrs. Walters interrupted. "Ignatius has Alzheimer's and sometimes he speaks gibberish."

But I didn't correct her. I knew what he meant by anak—"child"—because I knew Ignatius wasn't speaking gibberish. I still understood Tagalog. I also grew up watching TFC, The Filipino Channel, on television. It was an add-on subscription on top of regular cable, the international version of the flagship network in the Philippines.

As Mrs. Walters led me away, Ignatius gave up on the television and found a seat in a different chair.

"I hope this little fiasco doesn't scare you away," Mrs. Walters continued. "They are mostly well behaved." She had settled the argument between the other two residents. Kerry gave Richard one of the magazines with a swimsuit model on the cover, which appeased him, and he sat back in his original seat.

As I started for the door, Ignatius came up to me holding a piece of paper. "Anak," he said. "Your mother asked for these things." I unfolded it and read his writing in pencil. Bawang, luya, toyo, suka—garlic, ginger, soy sauce, and vinegar—the basis for many Filipino dishes. He must have been holding onto this list for a while, waiting for the moment his actual son came back for him.

"Okay," I told him. "I'll have them when I get back." But I never did get those ingredients for him. My job was a physical therapist, not a grocery shopper. But I lied to Ignatius that day, playing it off as if I were his son going out for errands. Every time I saw him, I continued to lie, feeling sorry for my father's doppelganger, answering his call for anak.

★

Papa is carrying me around his shoulders. We are at the airport, setting our things down in plastic bins, including our shoes, and putting them through the conveyor belt. The TSA agent says we have to go through the metal detector one at a time. So Papa sets me down before walking through. At the end, I can see Papa already gathering our things at the conveyor belt. Then it's my turn. The agent tells me to stop running and to walk through slowly. I follow the directions. But as soon as I get through the metal detector, I lose sight of Papa. I run around the conveyor belt, saying "Papa, Papa." But he's nowhere to be seen. "Papa, where are you?" Suddenly I'm surrounded by TSA agents. I tell them I'm lost and that I can't find my dad. But they don't listen. When I look up to see their faces, I realize the agents have none—they are blank, blurry voids of static. "Wake up, Francis," they say. "Wake up."

★

Layla inevitably sent me to a therapist. The doctor recommended a meditative podcast in addition to sleeping pills. I no longer made it all the way to the front lawn. Instead, whenever I began to sleepwalk, I went straight to the bathroom. The podcast's ambient running water most likely pointed my unconscious in the right direction—the toilet's siren. But at least Layla didn't have to get out of bed to fetch me from outside anymore. In December, there were already brief occasions of snowfall, but we were still waiting for the big one of the season. It was cold, dark, and unsafe. Having to reign me in every other night would not have been much of a problem, if Layla wasn't seven and a half months pregnant. I wondered if our baby would inherit my sleepwalking. "He better not," Layla said, already feeling the kicks and bumps inside her.

She also suggested a plan to help Ignatius. "Maybe he's like you," she said. "His body is here, but his mind is back home." In the same way my subscription to the podcast helped me manage my sleepwalking, she suggested that I subscribe to The Filipino Channel on behalf of Ignatius. Her thinking, she explained, was that if the resurgence of my condition was triggered by Ignatius, then solving his problem might also solve mine. She insisted on her plan, so much so she had already downloaded the TFC app on my tablet, which I brought with me to work to keep track of my patients and their sessions. It was worth a shot.

The next time I visited Eden, I called for Ignatius to join me in the exercise room. He needed some convincing, as he was always set on finding the right channel on the television. "You don't need the TV anymore," I told him as I led him away. "Here, look. I have TFC on my tablet." I sat him down on the chair and presented the device.

"Wow," he said. "Anak, this must be so expensive, so high tech—this must mean you finally got a job!" He smiled proudly.

"I'm a doctor now," I said, as if the scrubs I wore needed explanation, as if I wasn't his physical therapist. I hope his actual son was some sort of doctor. Though I knew he had children and grandchildren who lived nearby, I had no idea who they were beyond Ignatius' emergency contacts on file. His son's name was Cisco, short for Francisco—yet another coincidence. If Ignatius looked just like my father, did his son look just like me? If so, Ignatius' confusion went beyond Alzheimer's, perhaps beyond the natural laws of the universe. I had heard that everyone has one or even a few doppelgangers scattered around the world. Without any biological relation, these uncanny resemblances supposedly show the Creator's tired hand at work—a simple copy/paste job rather than divine originality.

As I examined Ignatius' body and motor functions—slowly rotating his arms and legs in circular motions—he watched a movie that looked familiar, one that my parents used to watch when I was a kid. "Look—it's Dolphy!" Ignatius pointed to the tablet screen. Rodolfo Vera Quizon Sr., or Dolphy, was the Philippines' equivalent to Charlie Chaplin. With a mustache that matched the silent film star, Dolphy embodied silliness. My father loved watching his films, and we always gathered around the television whenever one was on TFC. In this particular film, *Home Alone da Riber*, Dolphy hatches a plan to escape prison with some other inmates. One attempt involves the prisoners running towards the outer walls with long bamboo sticks, as if the sticks would hoist them up and over the wall like in pole vaulting. Some of the prisoners make it, but Dolphy doesn't go high enough—he lands face-flat against the concrete wall. Even that made me crack a smile and laugh along with Ignatius. "After all these years, he's still so funny!" said Ignatius.

Even at seventy-two, Ignatius contained all the youth and spontaneity of a teenager in his lengthy body. When I set the tablet down on the floor so that he would be able to stand and stretch to his toes, Ignatius had no trouble bending forward and reaching the ground. He was as nimble as Dolphy in his comedic prime; he could have cleared the prison wall in one attempt. Ignatius was, by all appearances, healthy for his age. But his memory was not as good, and I knew it would only get worse.

"Anak," he said. "How many more of these do I have to do? I want to go back to the television. I am missing my game show." The Dolphy film was still playing on the tablet, but Ignatius had lost interest, or rather retention, his mind falling back to routine. How could I tell him that *Game Ka Na Ba?* was already off the air? We still had a few squats to do, but Ignatius already proved his body. It was his mind that needed repairing, but I was the wrong doctor for that. I felt sorry for him—there wouldn't be much anybody could do for him. "Okay," I said. I helped him to his feet, like the loyal son I pretended to be, and returned him to the living room. Ignatius went straight for the TV cart, pressing buttons on the DVD player.

When I got home and told Layla about the day, her disappointment was as expected.

"So my husband will continue to sleepwalk," she said.

"Unfortunately so."

★

Papa and I are behind bars. He's calling for one of the officers to let us out. "He's just a boy," he says. We're wearing matching pinstripe jumpsuits with handcuffs on our wrists. "We did nothing wrong," Papa continues to protest. "My son is innocent." But no one pays attention. The guards are playing cards around a table, setting chips into a pile. Papa gives up trying to reason with them. He turns to me and holds up his hands. He has a strategy. With quick succession, he moves his hands in circular motions. In the whirlwind, one hand is magically freed. I try to do the same. I swirl my hands in sporadic circles, but the cuffs are resolute.

On my fifth attempt, Papa runs out of patience. He, in his lengthy, emaciated body, is able to contort his limbs through the bars, slipping one leg after the other. "Wait for me, Papa," I say. But he doesn't listen. He is tiptoeing down the hall, like a cartoon fox. Just as he is about to turn a corner to freedom, one of the guards at the poker table spots him. "Run, Papa, run," I yell. But it is too late. With batons raised in the air, the guards catch up to him and lash at him. I reach my handcuffed hands out towards him. I am crying. Though I see my father take each hit, all I hear is a live studio audience laughing. When the guards are through with him, they back away, revealing my father caked in makeup, a red nose, and an apologetic frown. "Wake up, Francis," the audience screams like a sports chant. "Wake up."

★

Once the weatherman announced that the big one was upon us, and the arctic torrent outside confirmed it, I called my wife and told her that I'd be spending the night at the Garden of Eden Care Home. Normally, Eden was my second-to-last stop as the assigned physical therapist. But by mid-afternoon, the snowstorm was in full swing. "I'll try to make it home once it's over," I said to Layla. But I knew from the weatherman that it would be hours before the end. "The doctor has become the patient," she joked. "You're one of the inmates now."

She wasn't necessarily wrong. Mrs. Walters showed me to one of the vacant rooms full of barebones furniture and bedding—not unlike a "furnished" college dorm. "Make yourself at home," she said, her dentures clattering more than normal as the facility's heating struggled to match the frosted Nor'easter swirling around outside.

On the other hand, Layla was staying with our neighbors, a young couple, like us, with already two children. "I hope you enjoy your sleepover," I said.

"You, too," she replied. Because who wouldn't enjoy a slumber party at a senior home? "And in case you start sleepwalking," she added, "don't forget your catheter."

Layla didn't get a chance to meet my father, but she would have loved his sense of humor. One of my last memories of my father was when he and Mama visited me in the city. I was in my fourth semester of graduate school, in between coursework and my second clinical. Mama, always the drama queen, took it upon herself to create an itinerary for their visit. Unbeknownst to me, she had booked tickets to a Broadway show for the three of us months before. "When in Rome," she said, as if their visit was a once in a lifetime opportunity (our hometown was in New Jersey, and Manhattan was just an hour drive away).

On the subway, Papa echoed my mother's words. "When in Rome," he proclaimed, wrapping one leg around the subway pole like an exotic dancer. He loved mocking my mother and her plans.

Mama tried to reign him in, "Stop it, Edmundo," shushing him as if he were a child, but Papa didn't stop. He kept singing "New York, New York" till we reached our stop. I hid my embarrassment behind a laugh, which he always worked hard to earn. Like in high school, when I first started driving, Papa slapped a Baby On Board sticker on the rear window of our car. "You are a baby," he said, "a baby driver!" I knew he only had my safety in mind. He showed his love through jokes and pranks. I loved him for that.

Now, the storm also brought up other problems at the care home. Mrs. Walters worried about the power, as many of the residents brought out space heaters to keep their rooms warm—despite Mrs. Walters' warning about fire hazards. "I'm going to burn in hell soon enough," Kerry said. She was one of my patients who kept complaining about their joints and followed my recommendation to keep warm. The other residents, who also retreated to their respective rooms, shared the sentiment of burning in hell before freezing to death. In the living room, there was only Richard and Ignatius. Richard was enjoying the magazines that Kerry left behind, and he sat comfortably in Donna's Italian chair. Ignatius was, of course, by the television.

"All to myself," Richard said. "Isn't this the life?"

"Did you ask Donna permission to sit in her chair?" I asked.

"What she doesn't know won't hurt her," he said.

I looked over to Ignatius and repeated his words, *What he doesn't know won't hurt him*. At least, with Ignatius' case, he won't ever know the truth that I was impersonating his son; his memory was ephemeral. *Ignorance is bliss*. That was what my own parents had in mind for me, too. When they visited me in New York, they had planned on telling me about Papa's brain cancer. He had been fighting the disease for a year, but they kept that information to themselves. Only after his death did Mama defend their secrecy. "You should have been focused on your studies," she said. "You didn't need to worry about him." Now, seeing Ignatius so determined to find the right channel on the television, I wondered about his own secret history with his family. Was his wife still alive? Why didn't she join him here? Why was he so determined to watch a gameshow which was already off the air even in the Philippines?

"Why does he want to watch television so badly?" I asked Richard.

"He likes to watch himself on the screen." Richard explained that when Ignatius first arrived at Eden, his family left him with a collection of home videos, keepsakes to help him remember his life before. "Mrs. Walters didn't like the way they spoke gibberish, so she stopped letting Ignatius watch them. We did also get into the habit of being too loud." All this time, Ignatius

197

only wanted to revisit his memories with family. Cruel—Mrs. Walters was cruel to rob Ignatius of those memories.

"The tapes are still there," Richard continued. "Ignatius just doesn't know how to play them." I went over to the TV cart to see.

"Anak," Ignatius said, "how do you change the channel?"

There was a stack of VHS tapes on the bottom rack, all of them labeled with a Sharpie marker: *Christmas '05*, *Cisco's Confirmation*, *Kimberly's Debut*, and *Game Ka Na Ba?* Cisco, I remembered, was his actual son, while I assumed Kimberly was his daughter. I figured the last one was what Ignatius had been looking for, not the actual TFC channel but a recording of his favorite gameshow on tape. "I think I found it," I told Ignatius. I switched the TV to the auxiliary channel, then made sure the VHS player had its connections correct. I placed the tape into the player, pressed rewind to make sure it played from the start, then let it play. I sat on the couch, in Kerry's spot, and Ignatius came to join me. Richard was satisfied in Donna's chair. When the up-beat, techno music started, Richard put down his issue of *Sports Illustrated* and paid attention to the screen.

Just as I remembered, the show started with Kris Aquino greeting both the studio audience and the audience at home. "Pilipinas," she announced,

"Game ka na ba?!" The audience, matching Aquino's energy, responded, "Game na!" To my surprise, not only did Ignatius join in the response, but so did Richard, who threw his hands in the air as if he were in the live audience. "That's what I'm talking about!" he said.

Ignatius, overjoyed at finally seeing his gameshow, echoed Richard, "Yeah, yeah. That's what he's talking about!" Aquino proceeded to invite the contestants to the stage—an elaborate, colorful platform that looked more like a Rubik's cube than an arena. There were ten contestants at the start, their names flashing at the bottom of the screen. I didn't expect that the last one would be Ignatius DeLeon of Pasig City, the same albeit much younger Ignatius who sat next to me on the couch.

"That's you, Ignatius!" I said. "You didn't tell me you were a star on the show."

Though his eyes were glazed with excitement, I didn't see any sign of recognition. To him, his younger self was merely another player. But to me, I saw the face of my father just before he died. His flat nose and thick eyebrows, his overall gaunt face brought to life with a smile. If my mother had seen this, she too would have been fooled into thinking Papa had been on the greatest game show in Philippine history. "Game na!" the young Ignatius yelled, and so did we—on the couch, years later, in a different country entirely.

"I see you've found the tapes," Mrs. Walters interrupted. She wore a pink bathrobe and held a toothbrush in one hand. I didn't realize how late it was. Out the window, it was dark, but the outside lights still illuminated the torrent of snow. I was prepared for her order to shut off the TV, or to make some kind of complaint about the noise. Instead, with a more passive-aggressive tone, she said, "Have fun," before retreating back to her office. Mrs. Walters could have been a character from a Stephen King novel, the night manager of a haunted hotel.

The game began with a series of Yes-or-No trivia questions addressed to each contestant. The capital of Portugal is Brussels—Yes or No? One of the Japanese cities bombed by the U.S. was Nagasaki—Yes or No? The X-Men can be found in the prestigious school of Hogwarts—Yes or No? One by one, the contestants answered, and every other answer was either right or wrong. With each wrong answer, a player was eliminated until only five out of the ten remained. Richard and Ignatius played along, too. Ignatius was correct every time—though it wasn't clear whether he accumulated this trivial knowledge before his live appearance on the show or if he merely memorized the answers from the recording. It was even more impressive that, in his condition, his memory retained these facts. Round after round of questions and eliminations, the young Ignatius advanced in standing, all the way until the end of the game when only he was left to answer the final question that would win him one-million pesos.

"If you win, what will you do with the prize money?" Kris Aquino asked him.

"I will bring my family to the U-S-of-A!" he said.

The camera panned to the audience. In the front row was a woman and two children, a boy and a girl—Cisco and Kimberly, I assumed. The woman had her hands cupped around her face, perhaps to catch the tears running down her face. She couldn't believe that her husband was this close to the million-peso question.

"This is for you Erma, Cisco, and Kim!"

I looked over to Ignatius sitting next to me, trying to catch some semblance of recognition. "Do you remember them?" I asked. But Ignatius' face remained entranced, eager to answer the final question.

"Pilipinas," Kris Aquino asked the audience one last time, "Game ka na ba?"

Together with the studio audience, Richard, Ignatius, and I replied, "Game na!" and hoped for the best.

"Your final question, Ignatius," Aquino began. This time, Ignatius would need an exact answer to win the game instead of just a Yes or No. "In 1903, this U.S. president revealed that God came to him in prayer and convinced him to annex the Philippines." I was ashamed that even I didn't know the answer.

"Theodore Roosevelt," Richard answered from his seat. "It was Roosevelt and his big stick!" he said with confidence.

"What's the right answer, Ignatius?" I asked.

He paused for a moment, just as his younger self did on the television. He had a minute to answer, and he let the timer count down. "Thirty seconds," Kris Aquino said. The young Ignatius seemed lost in thought, reaching through his mind for the final answer that would help his family emigrate to the States.

I didn't think Ignatius remembered. But as the audience began joining Kris Aquino's countdown from ten, nine, eight... Ignatius whispered, "McKinley." Then, as if his younger self on the television heard him, the younger Ignatius said, "William McKinley!"

"That is—" Aquino paused for dramatic effect, "correct!"

Then the screen cut to black. The recording was over before the celebration could take place.

"That's it?" I said.

"I won," Ignatius said. He got on his feet and started parading around the living room, like a kid on Christmas morning. He walked towards Richard and tried to pull him up from Donna's chair, but Richard wasn't having it—"Good for you, old man!" he said. Ignatius, still caught up in his triumphant victory, took a magazine from Richard's hands and started ripping its pages up into pieces, throwing them into the air like confetti. "Hey, hey! What's the matter with you?" Whatever joy Richard had for Ignatius quickly disappeared. Richard stomped around the room, shaking his head at all the pieces of bikini clad women scattered around the floor.

"I won! I won!" Ignatius said. "We are going to the States!"

"I think it's time to go to bed," I said, trying to calm him down.

I made sure Richard got to his room, where he saved some other issues of *Women's Fitness* and *Sports Illustrated* and laid them on his nightstand. Then I walked Ignatius to his room. "Anak," he said, "we are going to America"—not knowing that we already were, that he had been in America all this time.

After I said goodnight, I went back to the living room to pick up after Ignatius. Mrs. Walters would have broken her dentures in anger if I hadn't. Afterward, I thought of going straight to bed before realizing the television was still on. I ejected the tape, then saw the others stacked on the cart. I decided to put *Christmas '05* into the player.

The video played from the start, the first frame being Ignatius' son and daughter fighting for screen time. They looked not much older than they had been on *Game Ka Na Ba?*, so this must have been soon after they moved to the States. "Take turns," Ignatius said, "Cisco, let your little sister go first." Cisco carried his gift with him and sat alongside his mother Erma on the couch. Kimberly opened her present and revealed a bright pink dollhouse. "Do you like it?" Ignatius asked, to which Kimberly replied, "I love it!" Then it was Cisco's turn. The camera zoomed in on him, still huddled beside his mother. He tore through the wrapping paper and found a remote-control monster truck. "Awesome!" he said. "Now what do you say?" Erma said. "Thank you," their children said in unison. Was this the life he envisioned for himself? For his family? Did he make the one-million-peso jackpot count? Was his life fulfilled? I kept these questions in mind as I finished the tape and moved onto the others—*Cisco's Confirmation* and *Kimberly's Debut*—watching Ignatius' life flash before my eyes, insight into some parallel universe where my father lived further than his actual time.

★

Papa is lying on a hospital bed, his body hooked up to tubes and wires. But we are not at a hospital. Instead, we are on a stage surrounded by an audience with invisible faces. We are at the top of the pyramid platform. I stand at the contestant's position while Papa rests where Kris Aquino, the host, should have stood. The strobe lights change from red, blue, and green to a single white spotlight aimed at me. The upbeat music dissolves into a single, suspended hum.

"Game ka na ba?" Papa asks. The audience doesn't answer as they usually do—because the question isn't for them.

I know what he's really asking of me, but I refuse to give into the game. "I'm not," I say.

He asks again, "Francis, game ka na ba?"

I repeat my answer, "No, I am not. I don't want to play this game, Papa."

But he insists and answers for me. "Game na!" Papa lets out in one, exasperated breath; this time, the audience does join him, carrying the weight of his words, "Game na!"

"It's okay, Francis," Papa continues, "I've hit the jackpot. You're going to be okay." I don't know what he means by this. Was cancer like winning the lottery or being struck by lightning? Doesn't he want to live?

"Goodbye, Francis," he says. "You've won the jackpot."

How can I win if I'm losing you?

The lights cut to black.

"Goodbye, Papa."

★

The night of the Nor'easter was the last time I sleepwalked. After I had finished watching Ignatius' home videos, I made it to my room. But the morning after, I woke up to Mrs. Walters and Layla looking down at me, and I was shivering like a leaf. "The principal called," Layla said. "It's time for you to come home." I had managed to walk outside during the night, then laid myself on the porch bench.

"It really isn't becoming of a soon-to-be-father to spend the night outside, let alone during a storm," Mrs. Walters chided. Only after a series of apologies and a summary of my sleepwalking history did I get to go home with Layla.

At the same time, I didn't know that the night of the Nor'easter would be the last time I saw Ignatius. When I returned to the Garden of Eden Care Home after the holidays, he was already gone. "His son and family came after New Year's," Mrs. Walters explained. "They said it's time for him to return to the Philippines while he's still fit to travel. It'll help with his condition to return to some familiar place." She said all this with a misaligned smile, like a Bond villain—her dentures were upside down. She must have been happy to never have to hear Tagalog ever again. But I lamented that I didn't get to say goodbye. Then again, to him, I was his son. He never would have remembered Francis, the physical therapist who treated him all this time. Despite our regimented exercises, the routine never took root in his memory. Had I known, I might have told him everything, that I wasn't his actual son, that I was sorry I played along. But I was happy for him and his homecoming, his mind and body finally reunited. Back at Eden, Richard finally got his own seat, filling in the spot Ignatius left open—though that never stopped him from throwing a tantrum.

But since the snowstorm, Layla assured me that I hadn't gone out of bed unexpectedly—my subconscious autopilot was finally turned off. I no longer needed the podcast nor the sleeping pills, and there were no more zombified late night trips to the bathroom. Later, when Layla finally gave birth to our baby boy, I liked to think Papa visited him in his dreams. Our son, whom we named after my father, wasn't much of a crier. He slept quite alright through the night. He didn't inherit his father's ability to walk in his sleep. In fact, before he learned to walk, before he even learned to crawl, little Edmund merely laughed in his sleep.

ALONG CAME A STRAY

Moving back home was the last thing I had in mind. The house was built in the 1940s, a result of the postwar migration away from the cities and into the suburbs. A two-story, cottage-style home, the house was situated in a neighborhood just off the town's main street. Not so different from the rest of the houses on the block. When we first moved in, we had no furniture. I remember how excited I was, running around the empty rooms. Mirabel wanted nothing to do with me nor the house. She was five years older than me, had friends back in Manila, and was less enthusiastic about our move to the States. Still, bit by bit, new furniture filled the house. The living room looked like a living room, the dining room like a suitable place to eat. I finally got my own bedroom, which Pa painted blue. Mirabel's room was pink. Ma and Pa shared the master's bedroom upstairs. Now their room is still here but without its occupants.

Yet here I am, lying in the same bed of my childhood. Everything is the same. Still blue. The bookshelves full of accumulated summer readings, test preps, and comic books. Movie posters hang on the wall with years-old thumb tack. The last time I was here was before I left for grad school. Pa had already died, and Mirabel had married and moved to California. Ma lamented being home alone. "ABD," I explained to her, "All but dissertation. When I finish I can come home." I don't think she ever really understood what that meant. Nor did she feel consoled. "When are you coming back?" she continued to ask. I didn't know that I would be back only after she passed away.

A month after Ma's funeral, I invite Kelly Johnson to the house. Kelly was my high school sweetheart. After graduation, we split off. She pursued a degree in education and came back to teach at our high school—the same high school where Ma worked and made my teenage years unbearable. Of course Kelly showed up at Ma's funeral, where we reconnected. Now we are back in the house I've inherited, lying in the same bed I slept in as a teenager.

"Your mother wouldn't like me here," Kelly says.

"Not at all," I say. "But that doesn't matter much now."

"Don't say that." She hits a half-hearted fist onto my chest.

"She never liked us together."

"Do you miss her?" she asks.

"Yes and no. Like, how can you miss someone when it still feels like they can barge through the door any second? I can hear her cursing us in the name of God and every saint. Shaming us as if we are going straight to hell."

"Well," Kelly says, "that did happen."

She reminds me of the time when we were sixteen. One night, when Ma had a parent-teacher conference, I invited Kelly over. Mirabel was already away at college, so we had the house to ourselves. We overestimated just how long parent-teacher conferences took. Big mistake. As Ma was already through our front door, Kelly and I rushed to put our clothes on. But we were too late. Ma opened the door without knocking, which she did more often than she should have. Kelly and I were still in our underwear. She began shouting in Tagalog. "Bastos! Gago! Punyeta!" she yelled with some other curses I couldn't make out. The next day at school, Ma refused to make eye contact with Kelly.

"'I'm sorry, Mrs. Rodrigo, I'm sorry,'" Kelly says, out into the ether of this empty house, putting on her best performance of her sixteen-year-old self. "I don't think she ever accepted my apology. Even when I worked at the school, I could see through her pleasantry. I still felt the shame."

"I can't imagine being her coworker," I say. "I can imagine her as a boss, though. She should've been a principal."

"You know, I can put in a good word for you at the school. They're looking for a substitute."

"I'll think about it," I say.

Part of the reason why I continued onto grad school was to avoid that career path for myself—to avoid becoming an exact copy of my mother. She taught high school English, something she was really proud of. "Students in the Philippines know better English than students here," she said. "And I was taught by nuns and priests." She always held that above us, her fervent Catholicism and the fact that she knew better. But it also showed in her teaching. Making Kelly feel shame, for example. But if schools were so much better over there, why did she and Pa move us to the States? One of a few contradictions I would never understand.

★

Kelly nudges me awake. "What is that?" I rub my eyes before I hear the tapping.

"I don't know," I say. Kelly wraps a blanket around herself, then we get out of bed to investigate.

"*Ma?*" I say out into the dark.

"Quit playing, Jerry. I believe in ghosts."

If Ma were a ghost, this would be the last place she'd haunt. Her version of the afterlife would be in the Philippines.

We tiptoe into the living room. It's pitch black. Something is tapping against the glass door from outside. Squinting, I can barely make out a small silhouette.

"It's just a squirrel," I say.

"It's too big to be a squirrel. It's probably a beaver or something. Go shoo it away."

I walk over to the door while Kelly stays back—"Just in case," she says. I bend to get a better look at the creature shrouded in the dark. I start tapping back through the glass. Then the thing lifts its head up, revealing a set of glaring yellow eyes.

"It's a cat," I say. "It's just a black cat."

That reassures Kelly, who runs over to the door.

"So you're scared of a beaver but not of a cat."

"Cats aren't rodents," she says. "They chase off rodents." She tries to rattle the door open.

"You want to let it in?"

"It's freezing outside. No wonder it's been knocking on the door."

I turn the lock and slide the door open. After a quick *meow*, as if to say *finally*, the cat scurries inside. Kelly bends down to pet it, which the cat comfortably takes a liking to. She removes the blanket around her and sets it down. "It's a boy," Kelly points out. He curls up in the blanket, his paws tucked under his body like a loaf of bread. "You have to let him stay, Jerry."

"I thought black cats were bad luck."

"They're not vampires." She pauses to pet the cat again, who purrs and rubs his face against Kelly's palm. "Look, he's people friendly."

"Just for the night, then," I say.

"It's winter. This cold isn't going away any time soon." Kelly takes my hand, guiding it across the black fur on its back. It's still cool from being outside, but as I continue to pet him, he warms up. He stares at me, blinking like a child who's just woken up. Kelly explains that I don't have to keep him. "Just for the break. When I get back from London, I can take him off your hands."

How could I say no to her?

"Okay," I say. "I'll have to find a way to explain this to Mirabel."

★

For Christmas, Mirabel is bringing her family from California. She told me not to make it such a big deal: "Don't be like Ma and Pa." But since I was already out shopping for pet supplies for my new cat, which I still haven't told her about, I add some decorations to the cart. I don't go all out like my parents did. Just a few things: a plastic Christmas tree, a wreath to hang up on the front door, a few garlands to wrap around the barren walls, and some stockings, which I personalize with my nephews' names, Ewan and Michael. After all, I remember when Mirabel and I were growing up, we looked forward to the stockings. There were always presents under the tree, but Ma and Pa had their own strange tradition. After we unwrapped gifts in the morning, we found breakfast waiting in the stockings. Pieces of steamed rice cakes covered in sugar and butter. Puto is the Tagalog term, not to be confused with the Spanish expletive. Ma made them early so they would cool in time to be placed in the stockings. Maybe Mirabel will let us do the same with her children.

When I get home from the store, the cat is already at the door to greet me. I set down the decorations, planning out where to put every- thing. The cat rummages through all of it. At least Ma had Pa to help her. But I also remember how decorating or even cleaning the house led to many arguments. "Let me do it," Pa would say. Then Ma replied, "I can do it myself." But when Christmas morning came, it was as if they never argued. There was only genuine joy on their faces when Mirabel and I got excited for the presents, and when our own faces were stuffed with puto. When Pa died, Ma continued the tradition. She still woke up early to make the puto, up until Mirabel left for college.

When I finish hanging up the garland, I look for the cat. He had nestled his way into one of the stockings and made himself comfortable. "You're not helping at all," I say. I take a picture and send it to Kelly, making sure she knows how well we're getting along. "Cute," she texts back. She tells me it's snowing in London, just in time for a white

Christmas. Meanwhile, I have to put up with this black cat who up until now has no name.

★

"You named a cat Puto?" Mirabel says.

"You used to like puto when Ma made it."

"When we were children," she says.

I explain how he showed up one night, then how he snuck into one of the stockings and gave me the idea for his name. I admit it was Kelly who convinced me to keep him.

"You really do just let the strays in," Mirabel says.

"Stop that," I say. "Kelly's spending the holidays in London."

"On a teacher's salary? Are you sure she isn't seeing someone else?"

"She's with her parents."

She mutters something else under her breath.

"I always knew you had it in you," Charlie, her husband, butts in. "I just didn't think you'd get that kind of pussy."

I roll my eyes.

"Go unpack the rest of the bags," Mirabel says to her husband. He obediently follows.

The last time I saw Mirabel's family was under different circumstances. Both Mirabel and I had our fair share of tears during Ma's funeral. But for Christmas, we agreed to make it as cheerful for her sons, and for us, as possible. Adopting a stray cat, however, was not part of that plan. When they arrived, Puto was greeted by a pair of boys who just spent five hours on a plane. All that potential energy stuck in the air turned into immediate excitement at the cat laid out on the floor. Puto, fearing for his life, scampered underneath the Christmas tree. After being reprimanded by their mother for being so impolite, the boys came to me and said, "Mano po, Ninong." Mirabel, surprisingly, had kept up the tradition of children asking for their elders' blessing.

Now, Michael is on the couch watching television with his father. They're watching *American Ninja Warrior*. Michael clearly is more like Charlie. His hair is a lighter brown, almost a dirty blonde, and there are freckles across his nose. Ewan, on the other hand, has taken more from Mirabel. He has darker, brown skin and a flat nose. He's calmed down since the morning and is now playing with Puto on the floor. "I'm your big brother now," Ewan says to the cat in his lap. "You can call me Kuya Ewan." Maybe that's why I get along better with Ewan than with Michael. We are both the babies of the family.

★

Mirabel and I decide to cook dinner. When Ma and Pa made any special kind of dinner, they would make lumpia for us. But they made sure we didn't just get to eat the end product. They sat me and Mirabel down around the table. We'd each have our own plates, on which we rolled the pork filling into the spring roll wrappers. Between the four of us, we made a hundred lumpia ready within an hour. While Ma began frying some pieces for dinner, Pa cut up the rest and put them into Ziplock bags for the freezer. In the end, the lumpia was gone faster than when we made them. But it was worth it. I know now Mirabel might have wanted her kids to pitch in to make the lumpia, but perhaps the moment has passed, too late to pass on the tradition. It won't ever be the same as when she and I were kids, especially not without our parents around. "They can play with Puto," Mirabel says, coming up with an excuse, "to keep him away from the pork." Ma would have sat Ewan and Michael in their place at the table and personally taught them how to roll the lumpia. Ma would probably throw Puto outside.

"So is the cat supposed to be your and Kelly's practice kid?" Mirabel asks.

"We're definitely not at that point yet," I say.

"At least you've got someone," she says. She looks over to her husband, seated on the couch in the living room and watching the television, unbothered by her children chasing the cat in front of him. Charlie wasn't always like this.

Pa had died the summer before Mirabel left for college. At his funeral, Ma bragged about her firstborn going off to school in Boston. She didn't even consider that Mirabel might have wanted to defer a semester. "It's what your father would have wanted," Ma told Mirabel afterward. "Make him proud."

When Mirabel came back from Boston that Christmas, she wasn't alone. Charlie came dressed in a suit and tie and brought flowers for our mother. He asked for Ma's blessing, struggling to pronounce the simple "Mano po." He tried back then, *really tried*, and it paid off. Perhaps that's why Ma never approved of Kelly for me, who didn't try to connect with her. Charlie rolled up lumpia with us. He even attended midnight mass on Christmas Eve. At their wedding, Charlie agreed to wear a barong. I wore one too, and I walked Mirabel down the aisle in place of our father. She was genuinely happy with Charlie, so unlike the Mirabel who left us before her first semester. Instead of working through her grief for our father, she rushed toward finding new love. Maybe that grief is still somewhere inside her, if no longer for Pa then maybe for Ma. But we were never ones to talk about our feelings. Whatever her feelings are now, they're wrapped up with the pork filling of the lumpia.

"Michael, where's your brother?" Mirabel says as we finish the final batch.

"I don't know." Michael has just come back from the bathroom.

She gets up from the dining table and looks through the living room. "Charlie, where's Ewan?"

"He was just here a while ago," her husband says. "He was playing with the cat." He's had his eye on the television this entire time.

"Why are you like this?" she tells her husband, who now takes his time to get up from the couch to look for his son.

"Puto is gone, too," I say.

Mirabel looks at me as if I know where they are. I don't. I look through both the downstairs and upstairs bathrooms, and even rummage through my parents' room. Their bed is just as tidy as before, with no sign of anyone ever being there, not even a ghost. I go back downstairs and check the backdoor. Although it's closed, it isn't locked.

★

Charlie is on the phone with 9-1-1. While Michael waits with his father in front of our house, Mirabel and I decide to go next door.

"Hi, Mrs. Kennedy. I'm Jeremiah and this is Mirabel. We're Maria's children. I'm not sure if you remember." I've never felt comfortable speaking my mother's name aloud. I still don't.

"Of course, I remember you, little JemJem!" Mrs. Kennedy says. Mrs. Kennedy has the same long, silver hair—the kind that must have been blonde in her youth but is now a glistening trace of the past. The same blue piercing eyes that were just as welcoming as threatening. She yelled at Mirabel and me when we left our toys on her front lawn. But when the holidays came, she always brought over an apple pie she made herself. In exchange, Pa shoveled out her driveway and her part of the sidewalk. When we were teenagers, Mirabel and I pitched in. It was then that Mrs. Kennedy grew fond of us. I never knew if she was married or had children of her own. She hasn't aged a day.

She comes between me and Mirabel and hugs us.

"It's so nice to see you," she says. "I'm sorry about your mother. I miss her too."

"Mrs. Kennedy," Mirabel says. "We wanted to ask you if you've seen or heard a little boy or cat around. My son Ewan seems to have run off with the cat."

"I haven't seen either a boy or a cat," the old woman says. "What kind of cat is it?"

"A black cat," I say. "It was a stray that I just recently took in. His name is Puto."

"Puto? I know of a black cat but his name isn't Puto."

Mirabel and I exchange looks.

"Maria and I took turns taking care of a stray. Hold on." Mrs. Kennedy goes back inside her home. There's some scuffled movement throughout the house. She's rummaging through boxes and closets, looking for something. "I didn't know Ma and Mrs. Kennedy were close," I say.

"Me neither," Mirabel says. Eventually, Mrs. Kennedy reemerges from the house.

"We named the cat Elvis. You know, the rock and roll musician?" We nod our heads to assure her we do, indeed, know Elvis. "Anyway, for the past few years, Maria and I have been taking crochet classes over at the Elk Lodge. And at the same time, this little black kitten was roaming around the neighborhood. Your mother decided to crochet a blanket and leave out some food and water for him. Here's that blanket." Mrs. Kennedy unfolds it in front of us. It's bigger than it looks, a large white tapestry with a crocheted eagle imprinted on it. Red, blue, and gold threads make out the outline of its wings spread open. "It was Maria's idea. She saw Elvis perform live on television. *Aloha from Hawaii*. She based the design on the cape he wore on stage."

"It's beautiful," Mirabel says.

"Maria and I took care of Elvis whenever he decided to come around this side of town." Mrs. Kennedy refolds the blanket. "I'm sure you'll find him and your son soon. Elvis never gets too far." Her smile is reassuring.

"The police are here." Charlie comes over to tell us. Behind him is a cop car with its siren light on. "He says he'll take us around town to find them."

"We have to go, Mrs. Kennedy," Mirabel says. "Thank you for your help."

"Please, keep the blanket. Your mother made it. Now it belongs to you."

"Thank you," I say. "Merry Christmas."

We go over to Charlie who's already inside the car. He's in the passenger seat while Mirabel, Michael, and I are in the back. We unwrap the blanket again, showing Michael the eagle print. "So cool," the boy says. I should have thanked Mrs. Kennedy for being our mother's friend. It's nice to know Ma wasn't alone during all those years we were gone.

★

We find Ewan after a fifteen-minute drive around in the police car. Mrs. Kennedy was right. He and Puto made it about a mile away from the house and ended up underneath the town's Christmas tree. Mirabel spots them underneath the lights. They're snuggled together, Ewan nearly asleep and Puto purring. The cat had tired of trying to free himself from the little boy's embrace. "Not exactly little baby Jesus in a manger," Charlie says, chuckling to himself. The cop doesn't laugh, and neither do we.

"Ewan," Mirabel calls out. She tiptoes closer to the tree, which is in a little plaza in front of the town hall. "Ewan!"

"Be careful," Charlie says, "You might trip the alarms." He nudges an elbow to the cop next to him. Again, the cop doesn't budge.

"You're not helping," Mirabel says. *Sorry*, she mouths to the officer.

I tiptoe alongside her and motion for Mirabel to wake Ewan while I slowly unwrap Puto from his arms. "Ewan, baby, time to get up," she says, very unlike our own mother who would have woken up the entire block just to reprimand us. Ewan begins to blink awake, loosening his hold around the cat. Puto, breaking free, stretches out his paws toward me. "It's okay," I say, "it's okay." He jumps into my arms and I wrap the Elvis blanket around him. He rubs the side of his head against the cloth.

"I'm sorry, Mommy," Ewan says. "Puto kept scratching at the door and he really wanted to go outside. Then we got tired and took a nap." He gives his mother a hug.

"I know. You just wanted to play with Puto. But you can't just run away like that, alright?"

The boy nods. After his eyes adjust to the Christmas lights around him, Ewan comes up to me and Puto.

"I'm sorry, Ninong. I'm sorry, Puto."

"It's okay, Ewan," I say. I let him pet Puto, who is still wrapped warmly in my arms. Puto tolerates it. "I'm sure Puto forgives you, too."

★

We thank the officer, wishing him Merry Christmas, and decide to walk back to the house rather than be cramped up in the police car with Puto. On our way back, Ewan walks next to his brother and father. "You got in trouble," Michael teases.

"No I didn't," Ewan says.

They begin bickering about what happened. Michael begins to complain about how tired his legs have gotten searching for his younger brother. "It's all Ewan's fault."

"If you don't quit fighting with each other," Charlie steps in, "you'll both be in trouble."

I let Puto down to go walk with them to diffuse some of the tension. He stays close to Ewan, brushing up against his leg, forgiving his captor for taking him hostage.

"Ewan's more like you than me," Mirabel says.

"What do you mean?"

"You got lost around his age."

I was four years old at the time, Mirabel explains, and she was nine. We had just moved into the house. Ma and Pa took us to IKEA for the very first time. It was basically a mall, and they had all this furniture around. So we started playing hide and seek. But I decided to hide for too long. Ma and Pa began yelling at her, "How could you lose him?" Then she began to cry. "They blamed me, can you believe it? They blamed a nine-year-old girl for losing their own son." After causing a scene in the playroom section, they heard an employee claim to have found a lost boy over the intercom. "'I won, I won' was all you could say when we found you again. I was mad at you for a long time," Mirabel confesses.

"I'm sorry."

"You don't even remember," she says. "You had a perfect childhood. You got everything you wanted. They loved you more than me."

"Don't say that," I say. "That isn't true."

"Yes, it is."

"No, it isn't," I say. "What if twenty years from now, Michael said the same thing to Ewan? Would it be true that you loved Ewan more than Michael?"

"No, absolutely not."

"Exactly. Ma and Pa loved you just as much."

"They had a weird way of showing it."

*

Our parents were incredibly proud people. When Pa died, Ma took on their pride for both of them. Apart from school, I don't think they ever really got a chance to see how far we've come. Ma was, of course, happy when Mirabel got married to Charlie. But Ma argued with her about moving to California. "How will I see you?" she said. "*When* will I see you?" It turned out Mirabel and Charlie would only visit once in the summer and once in the winter. I could tell those first few years without her were hard on Ma. We spent our birthdays without her, and Mirabel's birthday was relegated to a phone call and a present in the mail. Once Michael was born, Ma tried pressuring her to move back. "A grandmother deserves to be with her grandson!" I remember Ma yelling over the phone. "We're already settled here," Mirabel would argue. "This isn't the Philippines." Back there, my parents grew up alongside their grandparents and great-grandparents, aunts and uncles, cousins of cousins. The saying goes *it takes a village*, but family back in the Philippines was literally a village.

When Ewan was born, Ma again pleaded with Mirabel. But my sister made excuses until, eventually, she answered Ma's calls less often. Rather than stay a week over the holidays, she stayed a weekend. But I guess that's what distance does, and Mirabel wanted distance. The last time we were together—Ma, Mirabel, and me—was for Ewan's fourth birthday. We flew to California to celebrate at Disneyland, the happiest place on earth. But when it came time for Ewan to receive his grandmother's present, there was an even greater falling out between Ma and my sister. Ma had gotten Ewan four plane tickets to New Jersey. Her present wasn't for her youngest grandson, but yet another ploy.

"I can't believe you," Mirabel said then.

Ma was perplexed. "I don't understand the problem." Seeing Mirabel's disappointment, she turned to Ewan. "You like my present, don't you, Ewan? You'll get to see Grandma again! You, and your brother, and your parents, we'll be one big happy family!"

"No," Mirabel said.

"Babe," her husband said. "It's fine. It's a thoughtful gift. We just need to check our calendars—"

But it was too late. Mirabel had the plane tickets in her hand and she tore them apart. Ewan began to cry. Poor Ewan. How could he know the hurt Mirabel felt then? How could he know what Mirabel was running away from? Throughout our lives, we always knew what our parents were running *toward*: some vague notion of the American Dream. But what were they running *from*? What did they leave behind in the Philippines? Now we won't ever know. It's a secret they've taken to the grave. Maybe we aren't so different from our parents.

After she tore up the tickets, Mirabel took the car keys and left. We didn't know where she went. But when she came back in the evening, she didn't say a word. She went straight to bed, giving everyone the cold shoulder like the teenager she once was. The next morning Ma and I left to go back to New Jersey. Charlie took us to the airport while Mirabel stayed in bed. How could she have known that would be the last time we'd be together with our mother?

★

"You know you didn't have to give up the house," I say to her now. "The house was meant for you."

"Charlie's got a good position in San Diego, and—God—I wouldn't want to move the boys at such a young age. Remember what happened to us? I really don't need the house."

"You're already doing better than our parents." I don't know whether Ma and Pa ever considered how moving around would affect us.

"Yeah right," she says. "After what happened today, Ma is probably scolding me from her grave." I do an impression of our mother, butchering my Tagalog, which somehow still makes Mirabel laugh.

★

The morning after Christmas, Mirabel and her family are ready to leave. Ewan and Michael are the ones who wake me up in the morning. Puto is hiding under the Christmas tree again while the two boys chase each other around the living room with their new Nerf guns, which were Charlie's gifts to his sons. Mirabel finishes packing, their luggage already by the door.

"Why's Puto hiding down there?"

"Target practice," Charlie says. His wife gives him a dismissive look.

"You missed it," Mirabel tells me. "The boys were aiming the guns at him." I look over to the boys.

"Sorry, Ninong," they say.

"You two have really given Puto a Christmas he'll never forget."

I go over to Puto, nestling him into my arms like a baby.

"It's a shame our parents never saw you like this," Mirabel tells me.

"Like what?"

"A cat dad," she says. "You're good at it too."

Between Mirabel losing Ewan and me losing Puto, I doubt either one of us would've made our parents proud. But I take the compliment anyway.

"Maybe it's time we welcome a pet into our family," Charlie says.

"That's a definite no," Mirabel chides her husband.

On the drive to the airport, Ewan and Michael don't stop pleading for their mother to agree to a pet. "I'll consider a fish," she says.

"It's not the same! We want one like Puto."

"Well, we can come and visit Puto when we can."

When I drop them off at their terminal, I can't help but feel melancholic. I tell Mirabel I love her and hug each of them. The airport security tells me to move the car. Then they are already through the revolving doors, waving goodbye. I go back to my car, apologize to the guard, and drive away. I hope they visit again soon, if not for me then for the cat.

★

It's New Year's Eve, minutes before midnight. Puto is playing with the lights on the Christmas tree. I am on the phone with Kelly, telling her about what happened on Christmas. She's glad everyone's okay. "I'll see you when I get back," she says, "you and *Elvis*. That is a much better name." When she hangs up, Puto is still playing under the tree. He has managed to pull off a red ornament from a branch, playing with his reflection around the metallic sphere. "Elvis," I say, checking if he still knows my mother's name for him. He looks toward me before going back to the ornament. He still remembers. I wonder what memories of her he still has. If only cats could talk.

When we were growing up, Ma and Pa made sure we were awake for the Ball Drop on the television. "Turn on the lights," they told us, and we did. In every room. Pa brought out a bottle of sparkling apple cider and poured some into four IKEA "Godis" glasses. Ma brought out the paper trumpets she bought from the dollar store. When Mirabel and I were younger, staying up till midnight was a thrill. It was the one night of the year when our parents didn't reprimand us for being awake that late. Between the two of us, it was a challenge.

"JemJem's just a baby," Mirabel would tease. "He's not going to make it past eight."

"Yes I will!" I'd say back. I fought against my eyes and swallowed my yawns, determined to prove my sister wrong.

After turning on the lights, from the basement to the second floor, Mirabel and I joined our parents in the living room. The television was set to *Dick Clark's New Year's Rockin' Eve*. Neither Mirabel nor I knew who Dick Clark was, and I'm convinced my parents didn't know him either. It just became one of those "American" traditions that my family fell into without much thought, like buying bottled milk instead of boxed milk.

But one tradition that stuck with us from the Philippines was jumping as soon as the clock struck midnight. "Why?" I would ask as a kid.

"So that you'll grow taller," my mother explained. I never believed her. But every New Year's Eve, just as the countdown began from ten, nine, eight... my parents cheered us on to get ready. Three, two, one. We jumped. And we jumped again, reaching for the ceiling as if we would, in fact, grow an extra few inches in the coming new year.

Mirabel and I followed Ma and Pa throughout the house, trumpeting our dollar-store trumpets, clapping, screaming, up and down the stairs. It carried on for fifteen minutes or so, until Pa remembered the sparkling apple cider he put out, which was already warm. He downed all four glasses because, by the end of our parade throughout the house, Mirabel and I were exhausted, pushed beyond our 8 p.m. bedtime. As eager as we were to go to bed, Ma still chided us to brush our teeth. After a lousy, rushed job, we could finally rest. All the lights were off, all was silent. The house, and our family, settled into the new year.

But tonight, the television is off. There are no more of those traditions. No more Ma and Pa to tell us what to do, to rally us awake for the midnight parade. My sister has already gone back to California with her own family. I wonder if she makes Michael and Ewan do the same things. Turning on the lights and making as much noise as possible, as if to wake up every room of the house. Jumping at the stroke of midnight, as if they would grow taller than they would have if they didn't. I hope she does. As for me, I am alone. Well, there's also Puto. The last time I saw Ma, she looked so small. She was still plump, as she'd always been. But I towered over her then, nearly a yard above her. Perhaps, in the fifty new years of her life, she didn't jump as high as she should have.

But now I can't help but feel small. The house seems to expand in proportion to the stark silence. There is only Puto's purring as he sits comfortably on his personalized crochet blanket under the tree. Ten minutes pass. Then the countdown starts. Ten, nine, eight… I decide not to jump this year. I don't want to break Puto's comfort. Seven, six, five… I imagine Mirabel, putting on her best impression of Ma, telling her sons to get ready to jump. They can jump for the both of us. Four, three, two… As I imagine the ball drop in the middle of Times Square, surrounded by all the kissing lovers, I am curled next to Puto under the tree, thinking about whether to start calling him by the name my mother gave him, and lamenting the thought of unrecoverable time.

THANK YOU

I would first like to thank my workshop peers and the creative communities at Saint Peter's University, Seton Hall University, and the University of Louisiana at Lafayette, as well as the 2022 Roots. Wounds.Words Retreat for Storytellers of Color, the 2023 All Write, Columbia Writers Fiction Conference, and the 2024 Martha's Vineyard Institute for Creative Writing Summer Writers' Conference. They have not only seen drafts of my stories but also fostered the energy and mutual support that continue to invigorate my writerly life.

I express my gratitude to Wandeka Gayle, Deesha Philyaw, Veronica Montes, Emily Adia, and Theresa Hollnsteiner, whose comments and feedback were useful in successive revisions of individual stories and the manuscript as a whole.

I am thankful for my dissertation chair John McNally and committee members Randy Gonzales and Leah Orr who read this collection in its first iteration as part of my dissertation at the University of Louisiana at Lafayette. I am also appreciative of Sadie Hoagland and Jessica Alexander for their feedback and guidance during my time at UL.

To the fine folks at Sundress Publications, thank you for taking on this project and for accepting me among your awesome authors. I am especially thankful for Krista Cox and her guidance throughout this process, and for Samantha Edmonds and her editorial expertise.

Finally, thank you to Mama, Papa, Kuya Jerard, and Marianne—my family—whose love, care, and support are ingrained in me and my work.

ABOUT THE AUTHOR

Patrick Joseph Caoile was born in the Philippines and grew up in New Jersey. His work is featured in *storySouth, Porter House Review, Chestnut Review, Solstice Literary Magazine,* and elsewhere. He has received support from Roots.Wounds.Words and the Martha's Vineyard Institute of Creative Writing. He holds a BA in English from Saint Peter's University, MA in English from Seton Hall University, and PhD in English concentrating in Creative Writing from the University of Louisiana at Lafayette. Currently, he is a Visiting Assistant Professor of Literature and Creative Writing at Hamilton College. His website is writingsbypatrick.com.

OTHER SUNDRESS TITLES

Pure Fear, American Legend
Laura Dzubay
$20.00

Ruin & Want
José Angel Araguz
$20.00

Kneel Said the Night
Margo Berdeshevsky
$20.00

Cosmobiological: Stories
Jilly Dreadful
$20.00

I Am Here to Make Friends
Robert Long Foreman
$20.00

Unrivered
Donna Vorreyer
$17.95

Death Fluorescence
Julia Bouwsma
$20.95

Pork Fluff
Hsieh, Tiffany
$17.95

Still My Father's Son
Hikari, Nora
$17.95

The Parachutist
Hernandez Diaz, Jose
$16.00

Florence
Cooley, Bess
$16.99

Spoke the Dark Matter
Whittaker, Michelle
$16.00